# She's the One

by
Verda Foster
& B L Miller

SHE'S THE ONE
© 2007 BY VERDA FOSTER & B L MILLER

ISBN 10: 1-933113-80-4
ISBN 13: 978-1-933113-80-7

First Printing: 2007

This Trade Paperback Is Published By
Intaglio Publications
Walker, LA USA
WWW.INTAGLIOPUB.COM

---

CREDITS
EXECUTIVE EDITOR: Q
COVER DESIGN BY VAL HAYKEN (photography@valeriehayken.com)

# Other Books by the Authors

## Verda Foster & B L Miller

Crystal's Heart
Graceful Waters

## Verda Foster

The Gift
The Chosen
These Dreams

## B L Miller

Accidental Love

## Vada Foster & B L Miller

Josie & Rebecca: The Western Chronicles

# Acknowledgments

Thanks to Patty Schramm for her endless help and support. She has read the story ad nauseam and still comes back for more.

Thanks to Sheri and Becky for finding a place for us in their schedule at Intaglio. They made us feel special.

Thanks to Valerie Hayken for the excellent job she did on the cover of the book.

Thanks to Sue Fabian for editing our book.

Thanks to Tara Young for her proofreading skills.

Thanks to Carolyn Viega and T. Novan, who advised us on police procedures. Their input was invaluable.

Thanks to Vada Foster and Marilyn Edwards, who helped proof the manuscript.

Special thanks to all those who have taken the time to read our stories over the years.

A very special thanks to Fonda and Elizabeth for their support.

And last, but not least, we would like to thank Kathy Smith for her help and encouragement over the years.


A note from BL Miller

I would like to thank Patti for her support and help. I love you more than words will ever express.

BL

# Chapter One

Nicole Burke wiped her sweaty palms on her uniform pants and studied her reflection in the mirror. Her short red hair looked neat and tidy, but she pulled a comb out of her pocket and combed through it again for good measure. Satisfied with her hair, she turned sideways, checked her uniform for wrinkles, and nodded her approval. She was as ready as she'd ever be.

The first day on a new job was always hard, and she couldn't help being nervous. Leaving the department in Hastings to work in Presson meant more than just a shorter commute. After months of working second shift, she had to adjust her body clock to third shift, as well as integrate with a whole new group of officers. She had met a few the day before when she'd been given a tour of the station, and that night she would meet the officer she'd be riding with for the next six weeks.

Nicole glanced at her watch and took a deep breath. She couldn't hide in the bathroom forever. It was time to report for roll call. She picked up her hat, tucked it under her arm, and squared her shoulders. "Okay, Nicole," she said under her breath. "Let's show 'em what you've got."

"All right, let's settle down," the watch commander, Lieutenant Danko, said. He looked at Nicole. "Some of you may have already met her, but for those who haven't, meet Officer Nicole Burke."

Nicole nodded and tried to control the blush she felt creeping up her neck from. As her eyes swept the room an officer to her left caught her attention. She was the only other woman in the room, and sat ramrod straight, her face expressionless. Her short cropped hair looked as if it were chiseled from stone. Nicole looked down at the hot sheet and read over it as the lieutenant passed out assignments.

She found it hard to concentrate and kept sneaking peeks at the other woman.

Roll call ended, and through the process of elimination, Nicole concluded the lone remaining officer was her new assignment. The imposing woman walked over and extended her hand in greeting.

"Officer Burke, I'm Sergeant Laurel Waxman, your new partner. But I guess you've already surmised as much," she said, gesturing to the empty room. "Nice to meet you."

"Nicole, please. Nice to meet you, as well," Nicole said, admiring the rich tone of her new partner's voice.

"Come on, we won't catch any criminals standing around here." Sergeant Waxman handed Nicole the keys to the cruiser. "Let's go, Rookie."

"Right," Nicole said, moving to keep pace with Sergeant Waxman. They exited into the cruiser parking zone. She listened carefully as Sergeant Waxman explained the importance of doing a routine safety check of the vehicle at the beginning of each shift and made certain once they were in the cruiser that her seat belt was fastened before putting the key in the ignition. As she pulled onto the street, Nicole said, "I hope the heater works better than the unit I had in Hastings. I hate being cold."

"No worries." Laurel flipped the heater on high. "Here, we look after our equipment. Speaking of which, what are you carrying for backup?"

"I'm not."

"You should," Laurel said. "I can recommend some good models."

"I suppose a backup wouldn't hurt, but I don't really think I'd need one."

"Until the day when you actually do. Highway Patrol cop four counties over had her gun jam during a shootout with a perp at a traffic stop. She wasn't carrying. Must have been thinking just like you. *Policewoman Monthly* ran an article about it a while back. She carries one now."

Nicole mouthed a silent "*oh*."

"Lots of back issues in the break room. You should read 'em. Might pick up a tip or two that can save your life—"

"*Unit 105 and S109: Intersection Adams and Willow, disabled vehicle blocking traffic.*"

"Unit 105 and S109 en route Adams and Willow," Laurel responded to the call.

*"105 and S109 clear 2237."*

Nicole stepped on the gas.

"Hey, easy there," Laurel said. "This is Presson, not the Indianapolis Speedway. If it was an accident with injuries, they would've told us. Needn't cause one getting there."

"Sorry. My FTO in Hastings said we should get there as quickly as possible." Nicole slowed the patrol car to just a few miles over the limit.

"A police car isn't a license to drive recklessly. Think about your actions. You know people run stop signs on these side streets. You were driving too fast to stop if one did. That's a nice big lawsuit waiting to happen."

Nicole gripped the steering wheel tight as she turned the corner onto Adams Street. Two disabled vehicles were blocking the intersection ahead. "At least it didn't happen in the middle of rush hour."

"Oh, no? See that big building on the corner? In about twenty minutes, six hundred moonlight-madness bingo players are gonna spill out, and where do you think half of them will be headed?"

"That's not good," Nicole said, imagining what a scene like that would be. She pulled over to the side of the road behind the accident while Laurel called in for a wrecker.

"What are you waiting for? It's your show, Officer Burke."

They exited the cruiser, and Nicole's nervousness at having a sergeant watching her faded as she took charge of the situation. A routine fender bender with no injuries, it took only a few minutes for her to calm down the rattled teenager of the fault vehicle and get information exchanged between the drivers. Only one car required a tow; the other was released from the scene. While Laurel cleared the remaining vehicles held at the intersection behind the accident, Nicole made her way back to the cruiser and breathed a sigh of relief. This one was in the books, and there wasn't a single thing Sergeant Waxman could criticize.

Turning one last time to survey the intersection, Nicole felt her feet slip from under her. What had looked like a simple puddle was water on top of an ice patch. She went down, soaking her hip and thigh with ice cold water.

"Hey, you all right?" Laurel called, walking the few feet back to meet her fallen partner.

"I can't believe I did that." Nicole took Laurel's extended hand and stood up. "Great," she mumbled, wiping her hands on the dry side of her pants.

Laurel smirked. "Nice job. What do you do for an encore? Take a dip in Lincoln Lake?"

Nicole shoved her hands into her jacket pockets. "Nah, the toxic sludge would keep me from sinking."

"That's true. You're okay, then?"

"Yeah, just soaked and cold."

"Guess that beats just being cold, huh?"

"Oh, yeah. Wet polyester in December…so much fun. Don't suppose there's any chance I can get changed? I have another pair in my locker, or I live about twelve blocks from here."

Laurel looked at her watch, then at her shivering partner. "It's as good a time as any to call for dinner break. If you're brown bagging it, we can eat on the way and call us out at your place. It's closer than the station."

"Great."

"There's some plastic sheeting in the trunk. Let's put it down, so you're not stuck with a wet ass all shift."

"Good idea."

Laurel grinned. "That's why *I* am the sergeant."

They rode in silence until they reached Nicole's house. Unlike the other 1950s split-level ranches that lined the street, her home lacked festive decorations and bright Christmas lights.

"Want to come in?"

"Yeah, sure."

Nicole caught her partner's disdainful look at the unshoveled path from the driveway to the house.

"You know in Presson, we write tickets for this. Twenty-four-hour rule."

Nicole flinched.

"Relax," Laurel said with an easy laugh. "I'm kidding. It's your driveway."

Laurel confused Nicole. She prided herself on her ability to read people. It's what made her such a good saleswoman at the mall, and it was a skill she knew came in handy in police work. Yet halfway through the shift, she couldn't get a sense of her partner. The rich timbre of Laurel's voice left Nicole even more off-balanced.

"I'll just be a minute," Nicole said as she entered the house. "Make yourself comfortable. The bathroom is down the hall on the right. Back in a flash." She ran up the stairs, ignoring the muffled barking coming from her brother's room. Grabbing a new pair of pants, she stripped down, sat on the bed, and wondered at her bad luck, certain Sergeant Waxman thought she was inept as hell.

Nicole dressed quickly and started down the hall, stopping at her brother's room. She raised her hand to knock when his door opened.

"What're you doing home?" Jim asked, using his bare leg to keep the struggling dog from barging past him.

"Sorry I woke you," she said. "I fell and got my pants wet, so I had to stop home and change. Can you put them in the dryer for me? Sergeant Waxman is waiting downstairs, I gotta go. See you in the morning."

"Yeah, okay," he said. He went to shut the door when one hundred thirty pounds of mutt came flying out and dashed down the stairs.

"Gomer!" Nicole yelled as she rushed after him. She reached the bottom step in time to see the large dog tackle Laurel and knock her to the floor.

"Oh, no! Gomer, get off her," Nicole said, tugging the dog's collar. Laurel struggled and tried to protect her mouth from Gomer's licks. "Jim, come help me!"

"I don't have any pants on," he yelled from upstairs. "Gomer! Come on, boy. Get up here. Just pull harder, Nickie. Gomer, get up here."

"You stupid dog, you're going to the pound if you don't move. I mean right now," Nicole said as Jim arrived and they tugged the large slobbering canine off Laurel.

Nicole offered her hand to the woman on the floor. "I'm so sorry," she said, mortified. "Gomer's too friendly for his own good."

"What is that thing, a moose?" Laurel asked as Nicole helped her up.

"Almost. He's Saint Bernard, Chow, husky, and who knows what else. I'm really, really very sorry about this."

"No harm, Burke." Laurel looked at Jim and smiled. "Thanks for helping rescue me."

Nicole noticed the smile and breathed a sigh of relief that the sergeant didn't seem to be angry. "Sergeant Waxman, this is my brother Jim."

"Sorry," he said, displaying a sheepish grin.

Laurel brushed off her uniform and shrugged. "A little slobber won't kill me."

Jim nodded and pulled the overly friendly dog toward the stairs. "Come on, Gomer. Nice meeting you, Sergeant Waxman. See ya in the morning, Nickie."

Let me clean up, and we'll get going," Laurel said as she stepped into the bathroom. "Oh, by the way, nice artwork."

Nicole saw where Laurel was looking and blushed. In the hallway was a framed print of a woman dressed in tight pants and a shirt buttoned only halfway up, allowing full cleavage to show. "Uh, um, it's not mine. I mean, it's Jim's," Nicole stammered.

Laurel shrugged. "Sure, whatever."

"Really," Nicole said, as Laurel stepped out of the bathroom. "Jim won it at the fair last year."

"Yeah. That's why it's in the common hallway, not *his* room." Laurel pursed her lips. "That's where I'd put it if I was him."

Without making eye contact, Nicole said, "We'd better get going, right?"

Laurel looked at her watch. "Unless you're trying to set a new record for dinner break."

"Um, no, I'm ready." She donned her jacket, and they were about to leave when a rather vocal yowl stopped her. "Puddy, I don't have time right now."

"Puddy? Your cat's name is Puddy?"

Nicole shrugged and let go of the door handle. "Short for Puddy Tat. She wants her evening snack. I guess Jim forgot to give it to her. It'll just take a sec."

"How could he forget something with a yowl like that?" Laurel asked while following Nicole into the kitchen. A large cat sat on the counter looking very put out and meowing loudly at being forced to wait so long for attention and more importantly, treats.

Nicole rubbed either side of the tortoise shell cat's cheeks. "Now, Puddy, you don't have to yell. You're not starving."

"Mrow?"

"You're spoiled rotten, you know that?" Nicole pulled out a bag of soft treats from the cupboard above the counter. "You be good, and Mommy will be home in the morning, okay?" She scratched under Puddy's chin until the cat began to purr, then put several treats down on the counter. "Good girl." She gave the cat a final pat on the head and turned to her partner. "I'm ready to go."

Laurel crossed her arms and looked at her watch. "Are you sure there's not a ferret here someplace that needs its litter changed? No fish to feed?"

Nicole glanced in the general direction of the framed print. "Nah, just a few skeletons in the closet."

"Isn't that the truth?" Laurel said as they readied to leave.

Nicole opened the door, and they stepped out into the cool December night. "Brr, feels like it dropped ten degrees since we got here."

"And winter is just beginning," Laurel said. "Come February, you'll think this is bikini weather."

Nicole laughed. "When pigs sprout wings and fly."

"No pig jokes. We're cops."

"So I guess we don't bring home the bacon, either?"

"Depends on who at the station asks you out."

"I thought you said no pig jokes."

"I did. Now let's get back to work."

The two officers patrolled the deserted streets in relative silence. Nicole glanced at the radio, then at Laurel. "Is it always this quiet in Presson?"

"Hardly." Laurel snorted. "Crime rises and falls with the temperature, and people aren't used to this arctic cold. Yet. Give them time to find their hats and gloves, and you'll be sorry you said that."

Nicole clenched the steering wheel. Even the most benign comment earned her a rebuke from the sergeant, but being knocked down and slobbered on by Gomer didn't seem to faze her. As Nicole tried to make sense of Laurel's confusing behavior, she watched the car in front of her roll through a flashing red traffic light. "I don't believe this. Doesn't he realize we're right behind him?"

"You'd be amazed how brain-dead some people are. I'll call it in." Nicole kept her eyes on the occupants of the car while she listened to

Laurel talk into the radio. "S109 at Polk and Maple. White Ford Contour, Adam-Robert-Adam, four-six-three. Two occupants."

*"S109 clear 2354."*

Once the car came to a stop, Nicole turned on the spotlight and aimed it at the driver's rearview mirror. Adrenaline made her heart pound faster. It was far from her first traffic stop, but it was the first with Sergeant Waxman watching. She didn't know why it was so important to make a good impression on her new partner, but it was.

Nicole cautiously moved toward the car. She glanced back, waiting until Laurel took backup position near the vehicle's right rear tire. When she approached the window, the driver lowered it. "Good evening," she said. "Driver's license, registration, and proof of insurance, please."

The driver handed over her license immediately while the female passenger rummaged through the open glove compartment.

"They're in here somewhere," she said, her head bobbing. "Where is it?"

"Move. I'll get it," the driver said, leaning over and taking the jumble of papers from the passenger's hands. She removed the registration and insurance card and handed them to Nicole.

Nicole took the documents and aimed her light on them. "You're not the registered owner of this car?"

"It's my car," the passenger said, fumbling in her pocket. "And here's my license."

Nicole compared the second identification against the registration. Satisfied she didn't have a stolen car, she looked back to the driver. "You know you failed to stop at a flashing red light back there."

The driver looked mortified. "I didn't see it. I swear I didn't see it."

Nicole caught the faint smell of alcohol and used her flashlight to scan the inside of the car, checking for any open containers. "Where are you ladies coming from?" she asked, glancing again at the documents.

The passenger piped up. "Bowl-l-ling. We were bowling."

The driver gave Nicole an apologetic look. "It's her birthday, and we stayed late. Everybody was buying her drinks."

"Yup," the passenger added. "I'm one hunner…one hundred percent drunk." She held up her finger. "But I'm not driving."

"I'm the designated driver tonight."

"She didn't have anything, offishur."

"Will you shut up?"

"Well, she did have some root beer, but that's it. She ain't shit-faced like me."

"Will you please shut up?" The driver looked up at Nicole and sighed. "She was singing to the radio. Loudly. I only took my eyes off the road for a moment to turn the radio off."

Nicole fought to keep a smirk off her face. "Well, Miss Thompson, wait right here."

Nicole walked to the rear of the car to confer with Laurel. Through the open window, an off-key rendition of *Copacabana* assaulted her ears.

"What'cha got?" Laurel asked.

"The driver appears to be sober. Her passenger, who is the registered owner, is completely inebriated." She glanced at the driver's licenses and the registration again. "They live at the same address. The safety inspection is expired by about three weeks."

"What do you want to do?"

"Well, I could give the driver a ticket for running the light and for the expired inspection."

"You could. But?"

"But I'd rather give her a warning if her record comes back clean."

Laurel nodded. "I would. Go run your check."

Nicole returned to the stopped vehicle and issued a stern warning to the driver. "You were lucky the streets were deserted tonight. I should be writing you up for running that light and for the expired inspection. I'm cutting you slack because you and your girlfriend were responsible enough to designate a sober driver. Have a pleasant evening, ladies."

The remainder of the shift was without incident, though Nicole knew such nights would be rare. Laurel took them through the patrol area so many times that by the end of the shift, Nicole had memorized the neighborhoods and every potential trouble spot.

Nicole sat nervously in the squad room as her partner read over her report.

"Are you comfortable with everything in here?" Laurel asked.

"Yes."

"Good." Laurel handed the report back to her to sign. "Very thorough. I'm pleased to see you place more emphasis on getting it done right, rather than just racing through it so you can go home."

Nicole signed her name to the bottom of the report. "I'll be quicker next time."

"Not at the expense of being accurate," Laurel said. "Don't worry so much about how long it takes to do the paperwork. Now make your copies, punch out, and go get some sleep."

"Copies?" Nicole opened and closed her mouth while she frantically tried to figure out what her partner meant. "I'm, uh...I don't think I've ever made copies of my reports. No one in Hastings ever mentioned it."

"It's another cover your ass thing," Laurel said. "Just like some cops like to use blue ink so they know when they see the report later that it's the original. Let's say you made a DUI bust tonight. Do you think you're going to remember all the details four months down the road if the case goes to trial? What are you going to do if the paperwork gets lost or misfiled? It shouldn't, but trust me, it happens. It's happened to me, so now I keep copies."

"I'll go make my copy."

"You don't have to take every one of my suggestions, you know," Laurel said.

"I know. But it makes sense. I appreciate any tips that help. Thanks." Nicole saw another officer enter the room and frowned. "Oh, great."

"What?"

"See that guy there?"

"Who? Officer Smythe?"

"Yeah. He's the bacon I definitely don't want to bring home. He asked me out in the parking lot before shift."

"Threaten to turn him in for sexual harassment, and he'll leave you alone," Laurel said with a laugh.

"Does that really work?"

"No, but it's always worth a try."

"I told him no. Besides, I've had enough with dating people from work." She tapped the report in her hand. "I'd better get this copied and turned in. See you tonight."

After Nicole left, Laurel realized how late it was and decided to wait around and visit with her sister. She picked up two coffees from the break room and headed upstairs. Balancing the cups in one hand, she knocked on the door labeled Lt. S. Waxman, then entered.

"Hey, Sandy. I come bearing gifts from the sludge machine." Laurel sat down across from her older sibling and handed one over.

"Oh, thank God. How'd you know I didn't get a chance to stop for coffee?"

"I didn't, but I figured I'd try to butter you up before you hear about the time sheets."

"I should have known you had an ulterior motive. What's on it?"

"It took Nicole a half hour longer than I thought it would to get the paperwork done. I'll arrange to bring her in earlier tonight."

"You'd better. The captain's already on us about extraneous overtime charges." Sandy took a sip of coffee. "This is horrid, but it's better than nothing. Did she need the extra time, or did your stable fees go up?"

Laurel scratched her cheek with her middle finger. "Leave my horse out of it. At least I get to ride alone with Cheyenne."

"Whiner. So other than watching paint dry while Officer Burke filled out reports, how did your first night of babysitting go?"

"Well, she drives like she's from New York. She's clumsy as all hell, and aside from the moose she calls a dog and the ugliest cat I ever saw, there's a twenty percent chance one of us will be alive at the end of the six weeks."

"What was her dog doing in your cruiser?"

Laurel smirked at her sister's puzzled look. "It wasn't. The moose was at her house."

"Oh? Care to explain?"

"It was lunch. She was wet—don't even. I stayed downstairs while she changed."

Sandy put her hands up. "I didn't say anything. You're the one who went to her house the first night you met her."

"Because she slipped and fell into a slush puddle, and we are so not having this conversation."

Sandy shrugged. "Whatever. Hey, I almost forgot, the itincrary came in the mail yesterday. Here, have a look." She pushed the colorful folder across the desk.

Laurel smiled and shook her head. "I can't believe you're going on a singles' cruise."

Sandy gave a Cheshire cat grin. "Mmm-hmm. Six days and five nights of horny single men looking for horny single women. They make them for lesbians, too, you know."

Laurel blushed. "I'd never be able to go on one of those."

"Prude."

"Slut."

"Maybe," Sandy said. "But at least I get it once in a while."

"Hey, Sis?" Laurel scratched her cheek with her middle finger again. "Right there."

"No thanks, I'll wait for the cruise."

# Chapter Two

Nicole winced when she opened the door and was greeted by music blaring loud enough to wake the dead. Jim was lounging on the couch listening to the stereo. "You might want to turn that up," she shouted. "I don't think they can hear it in the next county."

Jim got up and shut off the stereo. "Very funny." He followed Nicole to the kitchen. "Other than the Gomer fiasco, how went your night?"

"Miserable." Nicole walked over to the counter that separated the kitchen and living room and dropped her keys. "The soda machine ate my quarters, I almost had to write myself a speeding ticket, and to top it off, I got hit on by a guy on my shift."

Jim whooped. "Boy is he barking up the wrong tree. Did you tell him you're gay?"

"I think I'll keep that little bit of information to myself. I don't know if any of my coworkers are homophobic, and I have to depend on them to back me up."

"Even from your new partner? She rocks."

"Except when she's dressing me down. She didn't get mad after Gomer mauled her last night, but I may kill you."

"I'm sorry. You know how fast Gomer can be when he wants something. Let me make it up to you. Sit down and I'll whip up some breakfast."

Nicole looked at her watch. "Aren't you going to be late for school?"

"I'm skipping first period, so I can spend time with you. I don't have another class until third period. Don't worry, I'm not dodging a test or anything like that."

Nicole debated it for a moment, then sat at the kitchen table. "I could use something to eat. Do you need a note?"

"It helps. I've already got one unexcused absence this semester."

"When?"

"Um, back in October?" He thought about it for a second. "Yeah, October. No biggie."

Nicole watched Jim rummage through the refrigerator. "You're getting better at keeping things from me," she said, yawning and rubbing her eyes. "Oh, man, what a night."

Jim cracked two eggs into the frying pan. "I'll tell you this, your new partner can cuff me anytime. She's gorgeous."

Nicole was tempted to add that Laurel could cuff her, too, but instead she said, "Don't even think about it. She's too old for you."

"I like older women. Or are you just saying that to keep her for yourself?"

"Don't be silly. You know I'm never going to date anyone I work with ever again."

"Well, since you don't go anywhere to meet anyone other than work, I guess you're going to be single for a long time."

"Better than making another mistake."

"If you say so," Jim said as he frowned at the skillet. "Hope you wanted your yolks broken."

"Do I ever get them any other way from you?"

He chuckled and put two slices of bread in the toaster. "I'm thinking of pork chops for dinner tonight."

"Sounds good. We haven't had them for a while." Looking down at the table, she thought about how many other things they had missed since she joined the police force. "Jim? Do you feel as if I've been neglecting you?"

"Get a grip. I'm not a little kid anymore, Nickie. Christ, I've had more dates and girlfriends than you have."

"Maybe we should go do something together on my day off," she said, not responding to the ongoing joke between them. "Take in a movie or something."

Jim handed her a glass of orange juice. "I can see movies on my own or with my friends. You don't have to mother me anymore. I'm a grown man."

"You're sixteen."

"Yeah, an adult. You never have to worry about me, do you? Well?"

Nicole took a sip of juice. "No. You're very responsible."

"Then relax. Breakfast's almost ready. You worry about doing a good job and staying safe."

"I'm always careful. By the way, do you need any money for school?"

"Always," he said, causing her to laugh. "Nah, I've still got some of my allowance. I'm cool."

Nicole stood up and reached into her pocket, pulling out a ten-dollar bill. "Here." She pushed it into his hand. "Take Christine to the mall after school or something."

"Christine? I broke up with her weeks ago. I told you that."

"Sorry, you go through them so fast I lose track."

"I'm in between girlfriends at the moment. Kinda like you. I can give you some numbers if you want."

"I'll find my own girlfriends, thank you. I'm not into teenyboppers."

Jim slid the eggs onto Nicole's plate and set it on the table. "You realize this is the first time we've had Christmas here since Mom and Dad died? I want a tree."

"Sure. We can get one of those little tabletop ones and put it in the window."

"I want a real tree. You know, the kind that grows in a forest."

"It's just the two of us. We don't need a real tree."

"Yes, we do. We always had a tree before. It won't be Christmas without it. We'll move that chair and put it in the corner just like Dad always did."

"If we get a tree, and I'm not saying we will, you'd better hope Gomer doesn't think it's for him to use as an indoor toilet."

"I'll put a gate up to keep him away from it. I want a tree."

Nicole looked around the room. "Is there an echo in here?"

"Come on, Nickie. We have boxes and boxes of ornaments up in the attic, and Rob can get me a ladder, so I can hang lights up outside."

Nicole held up her hands. "Wait a minute. No one said anything about lights outside. We were just talking about a tree."

"If we have a tree, then we have to have lights. Dad always put lights up. We can't have Christmas at home without lights."

Nicole gave Jim a sidelong glance. "How many lights?"

"Well, we have to have some. Not too many, just enough to make it Christmassy."

"Not too many?"

"Of course not. You'll see. I'll make this the best looking house on the block."

Laurel pulled onto the dirt road that ran the length of Kulp Stables. Dust wafted up around her truck as she pulled to a stop beside her tack shed and turned off the engine. Cheyenne nickered as she unlocked the shed and stepped inside to pull a couple of flakes of hay from the top bale.

"Hi, sweetheart," she said in a gentle voice as she approached. "I told you I'd probably be late this morning." She laughed as the chestnut mare snorted and bobbed her head. "Yes, yes, I know you're starving, and your stall isn't as pristine as you like it." She tossed the hay into the big mare's feedbox and filled a small coffee can with oats.

Cheyenne was busily pulling bits of hay from the flake. "Here, let me help you," she said, pulling the hay into a loose mound and making an empty spot that she filled with oats. "See? I knew you just wanted me for food."

Laurel walked back into the tack shed and grabbed her rake and shovel, placing them in the wheelbarrow. "I'm late because I started riding with a new officer last night. Nice woman. I bet you'd like her." Cheyenne snorted and nudged her. "Eat your hay, and you can have the carrots for dessert." She braced herself for the stronger nudge she knew was coming. "Oh, all right, you big bully." She held out a carrot. "Now let me get this mess cleaned up, then I'll take care of you." She raked the soiled straw into a pile, shoveled it into the wheelbarrow, and grabbed an armload of fresh straw to spread around.

"Ah, the messes I get myself into, huh, Cheyenne? I get suckered into riding with her while she's on probation, and now I'm stuck for the next few weeks with a red-haired, blue-eyed dynamo who acts as if she lives for my approval." She patted the horse's rump, then reached in her pocket for the hoof pick. "Come on, give me your foot." She touched Cheyenne's fetlock, and the mare obediently raised her foot. "I swear I could tell her to walk backward and sing the national anthem, and she'd do it."

Cleaning the gunk from around Cheyenne's frog, Laurel smiled at how eager Nicole had been to please her. "It won't last long," she said. "She's only been a cop for a year. Still in that idealistic stage. Pretty soon she'll start bitching about how much paperwork there is and questioning me about everything." She applied Hooflex to the clean hoof and released her hold. Laurel moved to the other side of the mare and started the procedure all over again. "She's a lefty, too, did I tell you that? Throws me when I see her gun belt. I keep wanting to move her holster to the other side." She grinned devilishly. "I never looked that good in my uniform, I'll tell ya.

"Uncle Mark told me her parents died, and she's raising her brother. Now that takes a big heart." She moved on to the next hoof. "Do you think if something happened to Mom and Dad that Sandy would have taken me and Tim in?" She thought about it for a second. "Yeah, she probably would've, but that's not the point. Nicole is one of those people. You know, takes in strays and gushes over her cat like that furball was queen of the place. Puddy. She has a cat named Puddy Tat." She shook her head and smiled. "Ugliest damn cat you ever saw. Got orange around one eye and black around the other. Looks as if a drunken artist painted her. I guess it's a case of having a face only a mother could love." The mare snorted and nipped at her sleeve. "You stop that. I only have one more hoof to go." Despite the reprimand, she gave her another carrot before continuing her task.

"It's nice that she likes animals, you know. Maybe I'll bring her out one morning after shift, and you can meet her. Would you like that? Sure you would. I know she'll like you, but then again, who wouldn't?" She stroked the mare's neck. "You're just the best there is, aren't you?" She laughed when Cheyenne nuzzled her pocket. "That is when you're not bullying me to give you carrots." The morning passed as she continued to lavish attention on her horse and talk about the woman who had captivated her attention.


Nicole waited outside roll call, still embarrassed over her brother's rambunctious dog tackling Sergeant Waxman the night before. When she saw Laurel turn the corner, she straightened up and did her best to look professional. "Good evening, Sarge."

"Evening," Laurel said. "Ready to catch the bad guys tonight?"

"Absolutely. I'm sorry about Gomer last night. I should have remembered—"

"I told you not to worry about it. It's not the first time I've been bowled over by an animal," Laurel said. "Let me tell you about one call I went on. Dispatch tells me destruction of property, but they failed to mention it was a great big bull that did the damage. By the time I found out, I was already out of my vehicle. I had to call for backup from up by the light bar."

Nicole laughed at the mental image of this strong woman hiding on the top of her patrol car while a bull wandered around. "I bet you got razzed for it."

"Oh, yes," Laurel said. "Especially at Sunday dinner." She looked at her watch. "We'd better get rolling." They began walking down the corridor that led to the parking lot. "Did you remind Jim to feed Puddy?"

"I did."

"Good. I wouldn't want to get a call that the walking color palette was disturbing the peace with her caterwauling."

Nicole laughed. "She's not that loud."

"Pretty close," Laurel said. "And I thought Cheyenne was demanding."

"Cheyenne?"

"My horse."

"You own your own horse? Oh, man, I love horses. What's she look like?"

Laurel smiled. "She's a beautiful chestnut mare with three white socks and a diamond on her forehead. I've got a picture of her in my locker. Remind me, and I'll show it to you after shift."

Once on the street, Nicole headed toward the northwest corner of the city where they were assigned to patrol. The early December air was crisp, and she hoped the cooler air would mean less crime.

"Take a right here," Laurel said.

Nicole hesitated, slowing the cruiser down as they approached the side street. "Doesn't that take us out to Cleveland Avenue?"

"It does, why?"

"Just wondering." Nicole reluctantly turned the cruiser onto Elm Street, her speed dropping as she drove up the tree-lined street, coming almost to a complete stop several yards from the intersection.

"Something wrong with the unit?"

"Oh, no. Sorry."

"Pull over."

"Here?"

"Here." Laurel keyed the mike. "Unit 105 and S109, we'll be out at Cleveland and Elm."

*"Unit 105 and S109 out at Cleveland and Elm 0446."*

Nicole put the patrol car in park and looked down at her clipboard lying between them on the seat. "I'm sorry about that. It won't happen again."

"You want to tell me what it is about this area that has you looking as if you lost your best friend?" Laurel asked, her smoky voice gentle.

Nicole put her hands on the steering wheel and took several breaths before answering. "This is where my parents died. They..." she paused a moment to compose herself. "They were driving down Cleveland when a kid out joyriding ran the light and...." She didn't finish the sentence. "I hate this intersection."

"How long ago was that?"

"A little over seven years." She shook her head. "You'd think I'd be over it by now."

"I wouldn't think that. I can't imagine losing my parents like that."

Nicole sat silently for a minute before releasing a deep breath. "I'm ready."

"You sure?"

"Yeah." She looked over at Laurel. "Thanks." Nicole put the cruiser into gear and passed through the intersection that she had avoided for so many years.

Laurel stalled her truck halfway up her parents' cobblestone driveway. "Come on, Bertha," she said, starting the twenty-year-old pickup and easing it behind her father's gold sedan. Laurel's cell phone rang just as she was about to get out of the truck. She glanced at the caller ID before she answered. "Hi, Deb. You caught me as I was just about to go into my folks' house. What's up?"

"I was just wondering how things are going with Nicole Burke."

"Things are going pretty well," Laurel answered. "Why the sudden interest in Nicole Burke?"

"Why?" Debbie asked. "She's adorable, that's why. Just your type."

"You can't be serious." Laurel's brow furrowed. "I know better than to make a play for a subordinate. No sexual harassment suits for this gal, thank you very much."

"You're her partner not her supervisor."

"I outrank her." Laurel shook her head, even though the woman at the other end could not see her. "Your matchmaking skills are legendary, but I'll pass."

"You've been alone way too long, girl. You need to live a little. Just because Sandy can't find her perfect match doesn't mean you're going to end up single forever, too."

"I have higher standards than my sister, and those standards include that I don't go jumping into bed with every pretty woman I see. I'm her temporary partner, nothing more."

"Your loss," Debbie said. "I'm telling you, Laurel, my gaydar rang a three-bell alarm when I met her."

"Give it up, Deb. I'm not interested. And don't you dare try to set up anything from her end, either."

"Okay, but like I said before, your loss. Talk to you later."

"Yeah, later," Laurel said as she got out of the truck and started up the drive.

"Damn, I'm tired." Since every Sunday was family day at the Waxman house, Laurel knew the front door was unlocked and went inside to find her mother in her customary place—the kitchen. "Hi, Ma."

"Hello, dear, how was your week?" Elizabeth Waxman asked, leaning her cheek out to receive a kiss as her daughter passed.

"Tiring." Laurel walked over to the cupboard and pulled her mug off the hook. "Cheyenne threw a shoe, I'm running on four hours sleep, and my eyeballs are about ready to fall out of their sockets from all the paperwork I have." She filled her mug with coffee and reached for the sugar. "You know we have a form to tell us which forms to use?"

"I know, dear. I heard it from your father for twenty years. After dinner, you should take a nap."

"Yeah, Ma. That sounds great." Laurel took a sip and grimaced. "Uh. Why didn't you warn me you made that flavored stuff?"

"You know I always make hazelnut for your cousin Greg and his wife."

"But you usually make it with the old machine, not this one."

"The old one sparked when I turned it on, so I unplugged it. I was just about to make some regular."

Laurel took another sip, trying to pretend she didn't taste hazelnut. "Good. I could probably drink a whole pot myself." She scrubbed her tongue against the roof of her mouth. "Well, maybe not this pot."

"Oh, move out of the way, Miss Finicky." Elizabeth reached for the carafe. "How are things going at work?" She paused and looked pointedly at her daughter. "Your sister, who happens to call her mother during the week instead of making her worry unlike *someone* I know, said you have a partner riding with you now. What's her name?"

"Nicole Burke. She hasn't been on the force long, but she shows good judgment and quick thinking." She started to take another sip, then reconsidered.

Elizabeth poured the flavored coffee into the carafe. "Really? Her parents must be very proud."

Laurel looked down at the mug in her hands. "They don't know she's on the force. Nicole's parents died in an auto accident a few years ago."

"My goodness, how terrible."

"Yeah, it is, and she's had to raise her younger brother on her own."

"That must be hard for her. Wait a minute. Burke? Doesn't your Uncle Mark mentor an orphan boy named Burke?"

Laurel nodded. "Yeah. Same kid, though he's hardly a boy. He's taller than I am."

"He must be a handful for someone so young."

"I don't think so. Nicole's something special. Hey, Sandy," Laurel said as she spied her older sister entering the house. "We're in the kitchen."

"Hi, Mom." Sandy shrugged out of her coat. "Hey, Laurel, when are you going to break down and get yourself a respectable truck instead of that beat-up old heap you drive?"

"I think I need lieutenant's pay for that," Laurel said as her sister joined them in the kitchen. Nodding at the carafe, she handed her cup to Sandy. "It's hazelnut, but Ma's making real coffee. I've had about as much of this as I can take. You drink it. I'll wait."

"Gee, thanks." Sandy pursed her lips before turning her attention to Elizabeth. "Mom, the house looks wonderful as usual. You and Dad always make the holidays so special."

"Thank you, dear," her mother said as they shared a hug.

"Speaking of special, you should see the new PDA I bought Timothy for Hanukkah. He'll be so pleased. So when is my baby brother coming?"

"He's not," Elizabeth said with a heavy sigh.

"What? He's not coming home for the holidays?" Laurel asked.

"He e-mailed me today. We expected him to be rotated out, but they extended his tour. He has new orders and is being sent elsewhere."

"Again? Where are they sending him this time?" Sandy asked.

"Reykjavik."

"Great. Another country I can't spell."

"I-C-E-L-A-N-D," Laurel said. "Reykjavik's the capital. And you can't spell lieutenant unless it's abbreviated."

"At least I am one."

"Girls! Enough. Laurel, stop picking on your sister."

"But, Ma, she started it."

"Did not."

"Did too." Laurel crossed her arms.

"Ah, I see my girls are getting along as well as ever," Brian Waxman said as he entered the room.

"Hi, Dad," the sisters said in unison.

"The two of them," Elizabeth said. "I swear, Brian, they do this just to aggravate me." She pointed at the dining room. "Why don't you two make yourselves useful by setting the table instead of trying to turn the rest of my hair gray?"

"I'll do plates if you do the silverware," Laurel offered.

The sisters went to the dining room and began setting the oval adult table and the smaller kids' table.

"All joking aside," Laurel said. "It really sucks Tim won't be home for Hanukkah."

"I know. But at least up there, all we have to worry about are polar bears and frostbite."

"I can see why they made you a lieutenant. By the way, there are no polar bears in Iceland."

"How do you know these things?" Sandy asked. "Better yet, why do you know these things?"

Laurel gave a smug look. "I read...and not *Buff Men Monthly*."

"Speaking of buff, what do you think of Nicole Burke?" Sandy asked as they moved around the table.

Laurel shrugged. "Hard to tell."

"Who are you kidding? You know a good cop from a bad cop a mile away. You've ridden with her for three nights."

Laurel ran her finger over the edge of the plate, absently noting the old gold leaf was wearing away. "She's a good cop." Laurel set the plate down and moved on to the next setting. "She asks thoughtful questions, takes her paperwork seriously, and has a good rapport with people." She thought a moment. "Nicole has this gentle side to her that just..." She stopped, unsure where the thought was going. "I think she'll make a good cop."

Sandy set the utensils down. "Hey, you interested in her?"

"Are you kidding?" Laurel gave a short laugh and shook her head.

"*Laurrr*el."

"What?" Laurel put the last plate down. "I'm not interested, okay?" She reached for the stack of clear plastic glasses. "She's a rookie, Sis. She's too young for me, I'm not into redheads, and you're way off base."

"Am I?"

"Yes. You are." She shook her head and continued setting out the glasses. "You're as bad as Debbie Singer."

"Oh, no, don't tell me she's playing matchmaker again."

"Yes. Sergeant Singer has divined that Nicole is both gay and interested in me. Not that Debbie's spent any time with her or anything useful like that. She just sees young hot single redhead—"

"And frustrated, middle-aged dyke."

"Hey! Thirty-two is not middle-aged, and speaking of frustrated, how long until your cruise?"

"You know it's mid-January. I can't wait."

"If you'd saved some of your vacation time, you could've gone already instead of waiting for the new year."

Sandy shrugged. "What can I say? They give me vacation time, I use it, unlike you who hoards it like stale bread crusts. If they didn't allow rollover, you'd lose yours each year."

"You have no willpower. How long did you last this year? February?"

"Bite me. I'll have you know I used my last vacation day in May."

"Oh? Must be a new record for you." Laurel ducked the spoon tossed at her and laughed. "You couldn't hit the side of a barn from ten feet."

"Ah, but I'm the one who's going to get laid, while you get to sit home with your left hand."

Laurel set the last glass down. "I hope you get seasick."

"Are you two behaving?" their mother called from the next room.

"Yes, Mother," they said as sweetly as they could. A moment later, Elizabeth poked her head into the room.

"I can't believe you two kiss me with those lying mouths of yours."

"She started it," Laurel said.

"Did not."

"Did so."

Elizabeth shook her head. "My stars, children. When will you two grow up?" She started to leave, then turned back. "Oh, speaking of growing up, your Aunt Marion sent me pictures of Chrissie's fifth birthday."

"Oh, really?" Laurel said. "That's nice." She shared a commiserate look with her sister, both knowing what was coming.

"Three grown children, and do I have any baby pictures to show my friends? Of course not. Sandra, get the pie out of the refrigerator. Laurel, get the dessert plates down for me."

"Yes, Ma." Laurel walked over to the cupboard, sharing another look with her sister.

"My sisters are both grandmothers. All of my friends are grandmothers, even my hairdresser is a grandmother. You two are so wrapped up in your careers that you're going to wait until it's too late, then what are you going to do?"

"Celebrate not having to buy tampons each month?" Sandy asked, causing Laurel to snort.

"That's right, make a joke of it," Elizabeth said, giving them a stern look. "You're not the one who has to sit there and listen to her bridge friends oohing and ahhing over their grandchildren."

"Mom, we've been over this so many times," Sandy said. "You know I don't want children."

"You say that now. You mark my words, you'll regret that decision when you get older." She turned to Laurel. "And don't you even think about giving me that lesbian excuse. You know if you wanted a baby, there are ways to do it without being with a man."

"Mother!"

"What? It's true."

"I-I-I've told you I'll have children. Just not yet."

"You've been telling me that for years. Chrissie will be in high school, and I'll still be hearing that you're not ready."

"What about Timothy?"

"I gave him what for when I answered his e-mail," Elizabeth said. "It just breaks my heart that the two of you can't see fit to give me even one grandchild."

Brian made the mistake of entering the room, unaware of his wife's mood. "Where's the pie?"

"And you." Elizabeth walked over and poked him in the chest. "This is all your fault, you know. These two, they're just like you."

"What's got you so riled up?" he asked.

"Aunt Marion sent her pictures of Chrissie," Sandy said.

"Oh."

"Oh is right," Elizabeth said, crossing her arms and glaring at her two daughters.

Foster & Miller

# Chapter Three

N icole groaned at the not-so-gentle banging against her bedroom door. "Go away."

"Come on, Nickie. You don't want dinner to get cold, do you?"

She groaned again and put the pillow over her head. "I need more sleep."

"It's already 6:30. I figured you were tired, so I let you sleep an extra hour."

"Damn." Nicole stretched, then sat up and rubbed her eyes. "All right. I'll be down in a minute. Make some coffee, will you?" She yawned. "About a gallon should do." She heard her brother laughing on the other side of the door.

"Already have a pot waiting for you."

"Yeah, all right." She scrubbed her face with her hands, then used her fingers to straighten out her short red locks. Half-awake, she wandered downstairs and went to the kitchen where Jim was taking a plate from the microwave. "Thanks for the extra sleep," she said, flopping into one of the chairs. "How's the homework pile tonight?"

"You worry about eating." Jim set the plates down and joined her. "I got my English done while you were sleeping and just have a little trig left. No biggie."

She shook her head. "I'll take a quick shower after dinner, then we'll work on it."

"You just woke up, and you're going to be leaving in less than three hours to go to work. I'll figure it out."

"Don't argue with me. It won't take that long to get your math done."

"Okay, okay, geez." He forked a bite into his mouth and swallowed. "Oh, that reminds me. The picture money is due, and I need my payment for the yearbook."

Nicole braced herself. "How much is your yearbook?"

Jim used his fork to push his food around the plate. "Well…with or without my name in gold letters?"

She smirked. "I'll sign two checks for you, but don't go overboard, okay? We still have to pay for your class ring."

"Are you sure you don't want me to get a part-time job? I'll give up sports, and I can work a few hours after school during the week."

Nicole finished chewing and swallowed before answering. "I want you to concentrate on your grades. Earning a few bucks an hour at the hardware store isn't as important as passing trigonometry and keeping a good grade average. Besides, if you work after school, we'll see less of each other than we do now."

"But the extra money—"

"No. It's not open for discussion. There's no reason for you to work when you should be studying and spending time with friends and thinking about girls. Enjoy your youth as long as you have it." She stabbed a piece of meat with her fork. They'd had this conversation more than once, and she wasn't in the mood to have it again. "Dad wouldn't let me get a job when I was in high school." She saw his jaw clench and knew she was in for an argument.

"He wanted you to go to college."

"I don't want to talk about it, all right? You're not getting a job, and that's the end of it."

"You're not my boss, Nickie."

"According to Lincoln County Family Court, I am."

"I'm not a little kid anymore. I can work if I want to."

"You need working papers, and you know I won't sign for them." She took a few more bites and set her fork down. "Let it go for now. We'll get the dishes done, then get started on your homework."

He scowled and picked up his plate. "I just want to help."

"I know you do, but not yet. Maybe in the summer, okay?"

Jim took the dirty plate from her. "Promise?"

Nicole nodded. "But only if you get at least a B in trig."

"That's blackmail. Hey, isn't that a crime?"

"Call a cop," she said, taking the pan from the stove and putting it in the sink.

"I'll get it," he said, gently nudging her away. "You go take your shower, and I'll take care of the dishes."

"You sure? I should have enough time."

He waved her away. "Go. If you won't let me get a job, the least I can do is do the dishes by myself once in a while."

"All right. I'll be down in a few minutes."

"Let Gomer out, will ya?"

"Not a chance. I don't need dog slobber on my uniform. You can let him out after I leave. By the way, when are you going to change the oil in my car?"

"Ah, I'll do it tomorrow. Put it in the garage when you get home from work, and I'll get it done before you wake up."

"Check the radiator, too, please," she said. "It doesn't seem to be warming up like it used to."

"I'll take a look at it."

"Thanks."

"Hey, Nickie, if I can't get a job, can I charge you for changing your oil?" He scratched the back of his neck. "I seem to be a little short this week."

"I wish you were. Then all those jeans you got at the beginning of the school year would still fit." She did some mental calculations and sighed. "Use the ATM card but just twenty, okay? I have to pay the cell phone bill this week."

Nicole was barely through the front doors of the station when Sergeant Singer came up to her. "Officer Burke, how are you this evening?"

Nicole returned the pleasant smile. "I'm fine, Sergeant, and please, call me Nicole."

"Well, that's good to hear, Nicole. Getting along with Laurel?"

"Oh, yeah, she's great. I'm really learning a great deal from her."

"Good, good. You couldn't ask for a better partner than Laurel." She leaned casually against the wall, blocking Nicole's path. "We went through the academy together." She crossed her arms. "Yup, anything you want to know about Laurel Waxman, you just ask me."

"Thanks," Nicole said, unsure where this was going. "I'd better get going. I wanted to look over today's incident reports before roll call."

"You'll have plenty of time for that," the sergeant-turned-matchmaker said, pushing off the wall and putting her arm around Nicole's shoulders. "There's only the three of us women on the late shift, so we should get to know one another. Come on, I'll buy you a coffee."

Not wanting to appear rude, especially to a sergeant, Nicole allowed herself to be led to the break room. "I guess I've time for one cup."

"Wonderful. So I hear you live with your brother?"

Nicole nodded. She reached into her pocket for change.

"I've got it," Debbie said, dropping quarters into the machine. "How do you take it?"

"Black," Nicole said.

"Watching your figure?" Debbie pressed the buttons, then opened the door and handed Nicole the cup of steaming hot coffee. "I swear, all I have to do is look at a candy bar and I gain weight." Nicole politely laughed at the small joke and followed Debbie to a table. "If I didn't go to the gym at least three times a week, I'd be the size of a house. You know the gym's a great place to meet guys."

Nicole sat down. "I'm sure."

"Oh, do you have someone already?"

Nicole shook her head. "I'm getting over a bad breakup. I'm not really looking."

"That's too bad," Debbie said, patting Nicole's hand. "You know the best thing for a broken heart is a new man." She paused. "Or woman."

"I'm just interested in being a cop right now," Nicole said, avoiding the question.

"And that's just fine, of course, but I could introduce you to some very nice...people."

"Thanks but maybe another time." Nicole looked at her watch. "I didn't realize how late it was getting." She stood up. "Thanks for the coffee."

"Late? It's half an hour until roll call."

"Yeah, but like I said, I wanted to look at the incident reports. Thanks again."

"You're welcome. Anytime you need someone to talk to, feel free to call on me."

"Okay, thanks," Nicole said, knowing full well she'd never take the desk sergeant up on her offer. "I'll see you later."

"I can't believe how wide awake I am," Nicole said as they finished shift. "Usually I can't wait to go home and crawl into bed."

"You're getting used to being up all night," Laurel said, noting that the redhead did indeed seem to be full of energy. "You'll be dragging Thursday night when you've been off for three days."

"Are you going to visit Cheyenne when you get done here?"

Laurel nodded, concentrating more on the report in her hand than the conversation. "Every morning before I go home. Her Majesty doesn't like it when I have to have someone else take care of her."

"Horses are such gorgeous creatures. I'd love to see her sometime."

"You'll have to come out to the stables some morning after shift."

"Really? That'd be great. I'll follow you, and that way if I get tired, I can just drive myself home."

Laurel's head went up as the words sank in. "You mean today?"

"Sure, if you don't mind the company."

"Uh...No, no, that's fine." The offer had been made, and she couldn't very well back out of it now. "Do you have any street clothes in your locker? I wouldn't want you to get anything on your uniform."

"I have a spare uniform, as well as a set of civvies." Nicole grinned, a dimple appearing on her right cheek.

*Damn, she's cute.* "Oh...okay," Laurel said. "I have to go file a report. Go get changed and I'll meet you in the parking lot."

Laurel had only seen Nicole in uniform and was pleasantly surprised to see her in street clothes. Shapely curves showed through the faded jeans and the pale blue flannel shirt with the top two buttons undone. She looked younger, softer, and damn it all, sexier. Laurel forced herself to look at Nicole's face. "You ready?"

"Sure am. I can't wait to meet Cheyenne. Does she like sugar cubes?"

"She'd love you for it, but I prefer she has carrots."

"Would you mind stopping on the way, so I can pick up a bag?"

Laurel was touched by the thought. "No need. I have plenty in my tack shed. I buy carrots in bulk at the feed store."

"Cheyenne, I brought company today," Laurel said as they entered the mare's stall.

Nicole walked up and stroked the horse's jaw. "Well, hello, Cheyenne. Are you a pretty girl? Yes, you are. Oh, look how beautiful you are."

"I'll get you some carrots to give her." Laurel unlocked the tack shed, smiling to herself at the other woman's cooing.

"Would you like some carrots, sweetie?"

Laurel handed her the carrots. "Feed her these, and she'll follow you anywhere." Cheyenne immediately nosed between them in an attempt to get to her treats.

"Oh, no, you don't," Nicole said, laughing as she put all but one behind her back. "You're as bad as Gomer, aren't you?" Cheyenne quickly finished that carrot and nudged her for more. "Or more like Puddy. There you go." She patted the large jaw.

Laurel leaned against the rake and watched the redhead feed Cheyenne carrot after carrot. "You ride?"

"Me? I've never been on a horse. In fact, this is the closest I've ever been to one." Nicole smiled as the horse continued to nudge her. "Can she have more carrots?"

"You're being a piggie, Cheyenne." Laurel set the rake against the wall and retrieved more carrots. "Would you like to ride her?"

"I'd be afraid I'd fall off."

"You wouldn't fall off. Cheyenne's very gentle."

"Could you ride with me, or would that be too much weight for her?"

"I've never ridden double on her. I don't know how she'd react," Laurel said, feeling very nervous at the thought of riding that close to Nicole. She raked with more force than necessary. "I don't think it would be a good idea."

"That's all right. You ride her and I'll watch. Do you need some help?"

"No, I'm used to this, but I think she's had enough carrots. If you want to help, there's a big burlap sack in there filled with oats. In the bag is a can. She gets one can of grain and two flakes of hay."

"What's a flake?"

"Sorry, I forgot you're a novice at this. There's an open bale of hay in the shed. Just grab the end and a segment will pull off. Each of those segments is called a flake. "

"Okay."

Laurel loaded the soiled straw into the wheelbarrow, falling into a familiar rhythm. She was almost finished when she had a sense of being watched. Turning quickly, she caught exactly where Nicole was looking before their eyes met. "Uh…"

"Oh, um, are you sure there's nothing else I can do to help?"

Nicole's beautiful smile completely enraptured Laurel. "What? Oh, no. I'm finished here," she finally answered. "Just need to run this to the compost heap and I'm done." She paused another moment, trying to come up with an excuse to keep Nicole around longer. "You know, if you want, I can ask Sharon if we can borrow one of her horses. She's an old friend, and she and her husband own the stables."

"You sure she wouldn't mind?"

"I'm sure."

"Promise I won't fall off?"

"Promise," Laurel said. She really wanted to go for a ride with Nicole, but riding double was out of the question. No sense causing unnecessary temptations. "I couldn't put you on her big palomino, but her daughter Connie's horse, Grand Lady, is gentle as a lamb and only fifteen hands. Not nearly as intimidating as Cheyenne."

"You're sure?"

"I'm sure. Wait here, I'll be right back."

It took only a few minutes for Laurel to go check with Sharon and return with the buckskin mare. "Nicole, this is Grand Lady. Lady, this is Nicole. Be nice."

"She's pretty," Nicole said, "but not as pretty as Cheyenne."

Laurel grinned at the compliment and handed her the reins. "You hold Lady while I get Cheyenne ready."

Nicole's eyes grew round, and she clutched the reins tightly. "What if she tries to pull away?"

"Don't worry, she won't."

Nicole relaxed a little when Lady continued to stand quietly beside her. She watched Laurel saddle Cheyenne and bring her out to stand next to Lady.

"Up you go," Laurel said, and Nicole froze.

"She's so big."

"You don't have to ride if you don't want to."

"No, I want to," Nicole said. "Really, I do." She put her foot in the stirrup, and Laurel gave her a little boost. As soon as she was settled, she grabbed onto the saddle horn and held on tightly.

"You okay up there?" Laurel asked as she pulled the reins up over Lady's head and handed them to Nicole.

"I think so. I just wish they came with seat belts."

Laurel chuckled. "Now that'd be something to see." She mounted Cheyenne and turned to see that Nicole still had a death grip on the horn.

"Don't be afraid, she's not spooky. She won't take off on you."

"You better not laugh if I fall off."

"I won't laugh," Laurel said, though she was sorely tempted to by the look on Nicole's face. "You ready?"

"Sure."

"All right, we're going to follow the trail for a while, and when we get through the woods to the clearing, we'll open them up a bit."

"We'll do what?"

Laurel laughed and clucked her tongue to get Cheyenne moving. Lady's ears immediately perked up, and she fell in step behind the big mare. Nicole relaxed after a while and released the saddle horn, appearing to Laurel to be enjoying the feel of the powerful animal beneath her.

"This isn't so bad."

Laurel winked at Nicole. "Riding is addictive. You'll get hooked on it."

The path widened as they emerged from the trees, and Laurel coaxed Cheyenne into a slow canter. She turned in her seat to see Nicole's hands again clinging to the saddle horn as Lady tried to keep up. Lady's gate was smooth, and after a while, Laurel saw Nicole relax a bit. "There you go. Just relax and enjoy."

"You're right."

"Right about what?"

"I can get addicted to this.

"You've got to be kidding," Nicole said as she pulled into the driveway. Multi-colored twinkle lights framed the house, doors, and windows, while a half-dozen plastic decorations littered the front lawn. Large candy canes were taped to the windowpanes, and a giant

Santa cutout graced the front door. "I said tasteful, Jim." Shaking her head, she grabbed her bag and headed inside. She shrugged off her jacket and looked around. Several open boxes were scattered about the living room, garland and light strings poking out. The rocking chair in the corner had been moved, the empty space no doubt waiting for a Christmas tree.

"Mrow?"

"Good morning, sweetie," Nicole said, patting Puddy's head. "Did you see what Jim did? I don't remember having that many lights."

"Mrow."

"Yes, yes, I know you're starving. I'm sorry. I had to go somewhere after work." She opened the cupboard where the cat's food was kept. "Let's see, do you want tuna or turkey?" She quickly emptied the can, rinsed it, and threw it in the recycling bin. Gomer barked at the back door, announcing his presence. "You wait until Puddy's finished," she said, knowing the dog was warm enough on the enclosed back porch. She glanced at the wipe board next to the refrigerator.

```
Hey, Sis,
Like the lights? I told you it'd look great.
Gotta go to the store after school to pick up more
lights.
Pizza tonight.
Jim
```

"More lights?" Nicole shook her head. "Any more lights and they'll be able to see our house from space." She unbuttoned her outer shirt as she walked to the living room and flopped down on the couch. *I wonder if Laurel likes pizza.* Nicole debated with herself for a few seconds before pulling out her memo book and flipping through the pages until she found what she was looking for. She assured herself she was just being sociable as she reached for the phone. *Not as if I'm asking her for a date or anything.* She dialed the number and waited nervously for an answer.

"Hello?"

"Hi. It's Nicole."

"Hi. What's up?"

"I was just wondering if maybe you'd like to come over tonight. If you're not busy, that is." She cringed when she realized it sounded like she was asking Laurel out for a date, and hastily she added, "I finally got that catalog and thought maybe you could help me pick out a backup piece."

"If you'd like, sure."

"We're having pizza, but if you don't like that, we could get something else."

"What kind of pizza?"

"I like just about anything," Nicole said, a smile coming unbidden to her lips. "What do you like?"

"Veggies, no meats."

"Sounds good to me, what time's good for you?"

"I'm about ready to crash now, how about eightish?"

"Eight would be fine."

"Should I bring anything?"

"Just yourself. I'll see you around eight then." They said their goodbyes and Nicole hung up, still smiling. "We're having company tonight, Puddy."

"You sure you don't want to be alone with her?" Jim asked.

Nicole gave him a dirty look. "You stop that, or I'll make you take the lights down. It's not a date. She's my partner, and hopefully a friend, and she's just coming over to help me pick out a new gun."

"So why did we just spend the last hour cleaning the house? You don't clean like this when my friends are coming over."

"I want to make a good impression, okay? It's bad enough Gomer tackled her the first time she was here."

"And you changed your clothes three times, why? Admit it, you like her."

"As a friend," she said. "I'm not interested in anything else."

"Uh-huh, sure." He made a circle with his forefinger and thumb. "Just a friend."

She jumped when the doorbell rang. "That's her. Do I look all right?"

"Your hair is sticking out all over the place." He laughed when her eyes grew round. "Just kidding."

She glared at her brother. "Behave." She walked to the door, combing her fingers through her hair just in case. "Hi there. Come on in."

Laurel smiled. "Thanks."

"You remember my brother Jim."

"Sure, nice to see you again."

"Hey. Can I take your coat?"

Laurel shrugged it off and handed it to him. "Thanks."

"Doesn't look like the snow's going to let up tonight, does it?" Nicole asked as she led the way to the kitchen table. "Keeps up and we'll be measuring in feet, not inches."

"They're expecting another two inches before it's done."

"Glad you're not out in this tonight, Nickie," Jim said.

Nicole nodded. "There's another storm coming in Thursday. Supposed to be worse than this one." She stopped in the doorway. "Laurel, would you like something to drink? Soda, beer, coffee?"

"Beer would be good."

Nicole grinned. "Coming right up. The catalogs are on the table if you want to look at them."

"Whenever you're ready."

Nicole pulled two beers out of the refrigerator, totally forgetting a soda for her brother. "I was thinking about the Bursa you mentioned before, but I saw a couple of others that might be good, too." She sat down in the chair next to Laurel and opened one of the catalogs. "What about this one?"

"A little light on the firepower." Laurel tapped the picture next to it. "This one would be better."

"Really?" Nicole leaned closer to get a better look and caught a whiff of perfume. *Hmm, nice.* "What about this one?"

"That one would work, too."

"Oh, I'm sorry, would you like a glass?"

Laurel smiled and took a sip. "The bottle's fine."

"You sure?"

"Positive."

"Gee, I'd be happy just to have something to drink," Jim said. "Thanks for the soda, Nickie."

Nicole looked up at him and realized what she'd done. "Sorry."

"Don't worry about it. I'll get it. Pizza should be here in about ten minutes."

"Okay, fine." Nicole turned her attention back to her guest. They continued to look at the catalogs, Nicole listening carefully as her partner explained the pros and cons of each one. She was neither aware of Jim going into the living room and starting his video game nor of how much time elapsed until the doorbell rang.

"Finally," Jim said from the other room.

"Oh, here," Laurel said as she stood up and reached into her pocket. "Let me help."

"No, really, I've got it," Nicole said as she rose to her feet. She met Jim partway, handed him the money, then went to the cupboard to get plates.

"Mrow?"

"Well, look who woke up from her nap," she said as Puddy walked over to her. "You have food, and it's way too early for your treats." The multi-colored cat protested one more time before going to her window seat and flopping down. "Good girl."

"Hey, Nickie, I'm gonna eat in there and watch TV," Jim said, grabbing some napkins and taking the pepperoni pizza from the counter.

"Use a plate."

"Why dirty a plate?"

"Because I'd rather Laurel not think you're a total Neanderthal." Nicole set an empty plate on top of the pizza box in his hands.

"Fine," he said. "But you're doing the dishes tonight."

"Brothers," she said to Laurel when Jim left the room.

"Oh, I know what brothers are like. I have a younger one, too. The big bad Marine likes to pretend he was a perfect child, but he was always pulling pranks and driving Sandy and me crazy. One time, he put his pet hamster in her bed."

Nicole filled her plate. "Somehow I don't think Lt. Waxman appreciated that."

"Considering the way she screamed, I'd have to agree with you on that one."

Nicole took her seat. "So what'd he do to you?"

"Plenty," Laurel said as she sat down. "I think the worst was when we were in high school. I could still kill him for that stunt."

"What'd he do?"

"Well..." Laurel blushed slightly. "He brought a picture of me into school to show his pervert friends, and let's just say that a certain rear portion of my anatomy was showing."

Nicole almost spewed the beer she was drinking and had to cough before regaining her composure. "I'd have killed Jim if he'd done that."

"I was six in the picture, but still it's quite mortifying to be a senior in high school and have a picture of your naked ass being passed around the freshman class."

Nicole laughed and took a bite of her pizza. *I'd pay to see that picture.* "You want another beer?"

"No. I have to drive home later."

"Coffee? Take only a few minutes to make a pot."

"Don't make it just for me."

Nicole stood up, wiping her mouth with a napkin. "I could use some, too. Sugar and no cream, right?"

"Right. I can make it myself, you know."

"You're company," Nicole said. "Relax and enjoy your pizza. Do you play chess?"

"Only when I want to torment my older sister. No one likes to play against me."

"I have a nice chess set. We could play a quick game if you'd like."

"Sure, sounds like fun."

"Really? Great." Nicole finished setting the coffee to brew and grabbed another slice of pizza.

*Foster & Miller*

# Chapter Four

*U*nit 105, S109, fight in progress at 609 Juniper Place. Combatants reported as several intoxicated females."

Laurel keyed the mike as Nicole turned the unit around. "Unit 105 and S109, 609 Juniper Place."

*"Unit 105 and S109 609 Juniper Place 0054."*

Nicole had a sinking suspicion she knew that address. "You know where that is?"

"Between Eisenhower and Hoover."

Nicole cringed when she realized her suspicion was correct. She turned on Juniper and silently prayed that she wouldn't run in to anyone she knew at the bar. She pulled into the parking lot. "Should we call for backup?" she asked while looking at the blinking labrys over the bar door.

"Let's see what's going on first," Laurel said. "And by the way, watch your rear, Officer Burke."

"No kidding," Nicole said, realizing from the comment that Laurel was well aware of what kind of bar this was. They entered the bar and were immediately assaulted by the pounding beat of dance music. She motioned at the bartender, aware of the conversations ending and the eyes looking at her. "We had a report of fighting."

"Over there," the burly woman behind the bar said, pointing at the far end where one woman was holding a towel to her nose.

The crowd parted when they saw the uniforms, leaving Laurel and Nicole an open path to the woman. "What happened?" Nicole asked when she reached the victim.

"That dumb bitch doesn't know enough to mind her own business," the woman said as she dabbed at her nose and glared at another woman standing nearby.

"Joanne is my business," the other woman said. "She doesn't need a loser like you hanging on her."

"She can make her own decisions, you stupid bitch."

"All right," Nicole raised her voice. "You, sit down over there until I'm ready to talk to you." She turned back to the injured woman. "What's your name?"

"Lucy Batson."

A young blond with a pierced eyebrow moved close to Nicole. "I saw everything, Officer. I'd be happy to give you my statement."

"Good, have a seat, and I'll be with you in a minute."

"I'll be waiting."

"She's such a slut," one of the women standing around said.

"Yeah, but she's got good taste," another one said.

Nicole was grateful for the dimness of the bar to help hide her blush. "Um, Miss Batson, tell me what happened."

"I didn't do anything. I was just talking to Joanne, and Kim just went ballistic on me. She's Joanne's ex and doesn't want her to be with anyone else. A real psycho."

"Keep shooting off your mouth, bitch. I'll take care of you later," Kim shouted.

"If you don't want me to run you in right now, you'll sit there and shut up." Nicole knew she had to keep the lesbian love triangle from turning into the next World War.

"Ooh, real butch."

"Miss Batson?" Nicole said, ignoring the jibe. She took down the victim's version of events, then Kim's, then the witnesses'. From the corner of her eye, she noticed Laurel watching her. She also noticed the appraising looks Laurel was getting from the patrons milling around and wondered if Laurel even realized how good she looked in that uniform.

In the end, she determined the fight to be mutual combat and advised they could drop it or both spend the night in jail. The women may have been drunk, but they knew enough to let the matter go, after which the bartender banned both from the club for the next month.

"Oh, Officer, wait." A woman hastily scribbled on a matchbook and handed it to Nicole. "I didn't see what happened, but if you wanted to ask me some questions, here's my number." The woman gave her a wink. "Perhaps we could…talk or something."

"I don't think so, Miss, I—"

"Nickie?"

Nicole's heart sank. She recognized that voice. How had she missed seeing her in here? "Sergeant Waxman, I think we're done here."

"Nickie. It is you." A dark-haired woman stepped in front of her. "You're a cop now?"

"Yes, I am, Rita, and if you'll excuse me—"

Rita grabbed her arm. "Wait a minute. How are you?"

Nicole glanced over and saw Laurel watching. "Excuse me." She pushed past Rita, jerking her arm away.

"Nickie, wait."

Nicole didn't stop until she reached the cruiser. She couldn't believe the dumb luck and wondered how the hell she was going to explain this to Laurel. *Surprise, you're riding with a dyke.* "Damn it," she cursed when she saw Laurel speaking to Rita, who had followed them out of the bar. She turned her back to the scene, unable to stand watching any longer.

"I'll drive," Laurel said from behind her. Nicole shivered, from the cold or the gentle voice, she wasn't sure. Nodding, she reached into her pocket and handed over the keys. She tried to focus on her job, but her emotions were threatening to overwhelm her. Shutting the passenger door with more force than necessary, she pulled her hat down and crossed her arms tightly.

"Leave the door attached," Laurel said as she slid behind the steering wheel and adjusted the seat to her liking. "Call us in…Nicole, call us in."

"Unit 105."

*"Go ahead 105."*

"Unit 105 and S109 clear."

*"105 and S109 clear 0145."*

"Pretty busy in there for a Thursday night." Laurel pulled the cruiser away from the curb and settled into traffic.

"I guess," Nicole said, staring out the window. "Be a few DUIs coming from there tonight."

"You want to talk about it?"

Nicole felt her heart race. "Talk about what?"

"What happened in there."

She shrugged. "Jealousy over the same woman. Mutual combat. By next week, they'll probably be the best of friends."

"That's not what I meant. Rita?"

Nicole glanced out the window. "Just someone I used to know." She paused a moment. "What did you say to her?"

"I politely informed her what the charge was for putting her hands on a police officer and that I'd be more than happy to give her a tour of the women's facility downtown if she didn't go back inside and leave you alone."

"I wish we'd never gotten that call," Nicole said, feeling Laurel's gaze upon her as the car slowed for a traffic light.

"How long were you two together?"

"How did you know?"

Laurel laughed and pressed the accelerator. "I'm a cop, Nicole."

"Guess I don't hide things well."

"Well enough," Laurel said. "I didn't know for sure until tonight."

Nicole continued to stare out the window. "I'd rather it not be public knowledge at the station."

"No reason it should be. Be warned, though, everyone knows about me, so you might be tagged by association."

A little voice sang joyously inside as Nicole's suspicions were confirmed, but the stronger voice warned her to tread carefully lest she experience another disaster like Rita. "I think Sergeant Singer is trying to see if there's something going on between us."

Laurel shook her head. "I told Deb to leave you alone. Did she tell you about me?"

"Not in so many words, but she kept asking me what I thought about you. I got the feeling she was fishing for information."

"She is the eyes, ears, nose, and throat of the department grapevine," Laurel said. "She's also a self-proclaimed expert matchmaker, so watch out." She pulled the car into a well-lit parking lot and let it idle. "Call us in for dinner break at Washington and Elm."

Nicole nodded and called in.

"All right...talk"

"About what?"

"Rita."

"Oh." Nicole reached into her bag and pulled out an apple, looking everywhere but at the woman sitting next to her. "I met her when I was working at the mall." She took a bite, taking the extra moments to get her thoughts together. "I really thought I'd found Ms. Right when I met her, and everything was great for the first few months."

"What happened?"

"She couldn't handle me taking care of Jim." Nicole took another bite. "She wanted me to send him to live with relatives, so she could move into the house with me."

"She couldn't live with the two of you?"

"Rita wasn't into kids. Said being saddled with a kid would cramp her style. He was a teenager, for God's sake. It's not as if he needed constant supervision."

"So you broke up with her?"

"I had to. She wanted me to choose between her and Jim." She looked out the window, staring at the snowflakes falling on the cars parked on the side of the road. "I told her how I cashed in my college fund to pay for the lawyers to help me get custody of him. She knew I wanted him with me. I thought we had something special. I thought she understood." She shook her head. "How can someone who says she loves you do something like that?"

"Sounds like she hurt you very badly."

Nicole turned to see a compassionate look on Laurel's face. "She did."

"She never should have put you in that position," Laurel continued. "You were right to dump her. You deserve better."

Nicole looked down, pleasantly warmed by the gentle words. "Thanks."

"I mean it, Nicole. Don't worry about her. She's not worth the energy." She held out half of her sandwich. "Want half?" Nicole shook her head. "Too bad. Ma sent me home with enough corned beef sandwiches to last until the next millennium." They ate in silence for several minutes before Laurel spoke again. "I was with Theresa for just over two years." She took a bite. "Wasn't as bad a breakup as you had, but it was pretty rough."

"What happened?"

"We just grew apart. It's all right. We make better friends than lovers anyway."

"You still speak to her?"

Laurel nodded and swallowed before answering. "She moved to California last year, so I get an e-mail once in a while, but before that, we probably talked about once a month."

"Tonight's the first time I've seen Rita since we broke up. I…" She looked at Laurel, seeing caring and understanding in her eyes. "I couldn't even bring myself to go back to work after that. Hell, it's still hard just to go into the mall." She rubbed her brow, pushing the painful memories back. "One good thing came of it. It spurred me on to follow my dream to be a police officer."

"I'm glad Theresa worked in real estate. It would have been hard to see her every day at work once she moved out."

"You lived together?"

Laurel nodded. "For most of the two years we were together." She looked at her watch. "I think we'd better hit the road. Think you're all right to drive now?"

"Yeah." Nicole reached for the door handle. "Thanks, Laurel."

"What are friends for? Get out, take a few breaths, get your focus back, then we'll go catch some bad guys." They got out to switch places, but when they crossed paths in front of the car, Laurel reached out and touched Nicole's arm. "I meant what I said before. You deserve better than that short little snot." She continued on to the passenger side without giving Nicole a chance to respond.

"Unit 105 and S109 clear."

"*105 and S109 clear 0237,*" the dispatcher replied as Nicole settled into the driver's seat.

"Let's hope there's no more bar fights tonight," she said as she put the cruiser into drive. "I'm not in the mood to run into any more ghosts from the past."

"I can't imagine you have that many ghosts," Laurel said.

Nicole wondered how many ghosts Laurel had but didn't dare ask. "Not that many," she said. She pointed at the car in front of them. "Busted taillight."

"I'll call it in," Laurel said. "Unit 105 and S109."

"*105 and S109.*"

"Traffic stop 500 block of Elm Street. Blue Chevy Cavalier, one occupant. Oscar-David-Robert One-One-Six."

Nicole followed the Chevy to the curb as it slowed down, then aimed the spotlight at the rearview mirror. "Looks like a big fella," she said before grabbing her hat and stepping out of the car. She barely reached the rear of the Chevy when the driver's door opened, and the large man stepped out. She quickly pulled her canister of pepper spray from her belt and pointed it at him. "Get back in your vehicle, sir."

The man suddenly lunged at Nicole, and she sprayed his eyes with pepper spray. He howled in pain and blindly lashed out, cutting a deep gash in her arm with a box cutter. Pain burned across her left bicep, but instinct kept her spraying him as she followed him to the ground, stopping the spray only when she saw Laurel's knee against his neck. "Stop resisting," she said in as firm a voice as she could, aware of the blood dripping down her arm. She reached for her cuffs, knowing she had made a mistake by not drawing her weapon. "You're under arrest," she said, securing the handcuff around his right wrist. "Give me your other hand." She fastened the left cuff and stood up, holding her arm. She leaned against the Chevy; a rushing sound filled her ears as she watched her blood drip on the fallen snow. This wasn't a cut she could keep hidden. "Laurel?" She silently cursed herself for not being able to keep the quaver from her voice. She watched Laurel look from her to the drops of crimson hitting the snow and back.

"Sit down," Laurel said, the urgency in her voice mistaken as anger by Nicole. Laurel pushed a handkerchief over the wound and pressed Nicole's hand against it. "Keep pressure on it." Nicole did as she was told while the man continued to scream about the pain in his eyes from the pepper spray.

"Sorry." She pressed hard on the gash.

"Just be still." Laurel keyed her shoulder mike. "S109."

"*S109 go ahead.*"

"Officer down. Request an ambulance my location, as well as male unit to search suspect and transport."

Officer John Decker's voice came through the radio. "*Unit 702 responding to S109's location. ETA three minutes.*"

"*Clear S109. Ambulance responding to your location. Unit 702 also responding.*"

Nicole heard the crunch of Laurel's footsteps in the snow, then the sound of the patrol car's trunk slam, but she kept her eyes on the suspect, unable to face Laurel. The distant sound of a police siren began to fill the night as the suspect's screams turned into pitiful cries. "I'm sorry," Nicole repeated as Laurel removed the now bloody handkerchief and pressed a soft pad against her arm.

"Just hold this," Laurel said, wrapping Nicole's hand around the pad. "The rescue squad is on the way. Are you hurt anywhere else?"

"N-no. I'm sorry. I didn't see it." Laurel's hand covered hers, applying pressure against her bleeding arm.

"We'll talk about it later."

Nicole closed her eyes, fighting back angry tears at her mistake. "I should have drawn my weapon. I should have reacted quicker. I—"

"You can't change what happened," Laurel said as a cruiser pulled up behind their unit. "John! Bring your first aid kit." Within seconds, Officer Decker was kneeling next to them. "I didn't search him. The weapon's over there."

He gave Nicole a reassuring smile. "You'll be okay, Rookie. I'll take care of him for you." She watched as he roughly pulled the suspect to his feet and leaned him over the hood of the Chevy.

"Make sure you Mirandize him with a card," Laurel said. "I don't want him getting off on a technicality."

"Not a chance."

Nicole tried to pull away as Laurel covered the bloody pad with a fresh one, her latex-covered fingers brushing against Nicole's. "I'll be okay," she said. "Really, it's not that bad."

"It is that bad, and stay still," Laurel said. She keyed her shoulder mike. "S109, where's that ambulance?"

"*S109, ambulance is on its way. L104 is also en route to your location.*"

Nicole cringed at the thought of Lieutenant Danko coming to the scene. "Don't let them call Jim," she said, remembering she had him listed as her emergency contact. "I don't want him to worry."

"I won't," Laurel said. "Are you allergic to anything? Anything the EMTs should know?"

Nicole shook her head. "I can't believe this happened."

"You're going to be all right," Laurel said as the rescue truck pulled up.

Laurel headed right for Sandy when she entered the station. "I need to talk to you."

"And a good morning to you, too," Sandy said as she unbuttoned her coat. Noting the grave look on Laurel's face, she frowned. "What's wrong?"

"You didn't hear about last night, did you?"

"Did you just see me walk through the front door? I haven't even had a cup of coffee yet." Sandy stopped short when she saw the stain on Laurel's uniform shirt. "Is that what I think it is?"

Laurel nodded. "Nicole was injured last night during a traffic stop."

"Oh, God. Is she all right?"

"She'll be okay. Look, can we go in your office and talk about this?" Laurel asked, not so gently urging her sister toward the squad room. Once inside Sandy's office, she began pacing. "I screwed up."

"How?"

"I wasn't paying enough attention. I should have noticed all the bugs on his license plate and called for a felony stop. Any idiot knows you don't get bugs on a back plate. Instead, I let her walk right up to him. Before I could do anything, he was out of the car and slashing at her with a box cutter." She banged her hand against the tall filing cabinet. "I should have noticed a front plate on the back. I should have moved faster when I saw him get out of the car." She began pacing. "I should have been in position to get a shot off without her being in the way." She rested her fists on Sandy's desk. "She's got a three-inch gash on her arm." Closing her eyes, she shook her head. "You should have seen her, Sandy. She's there with blood running down her arm, and she has the presence of mind to get the cuffs on him."

Sandy put her hand on her sister's back. "Why don't you have a seat?"

"She's sitting there bleeding, and all she can do is say she's sorry for getting hurt," Laurel continued. "She didn't even realize it was my fault. If she hadn't put her arm up to block the knife, he could have slit her throat."

"Sit," Sandy said.

"She didn't draw her weapon. I know she had her hand on her holster as she approached. She always does." Laurel sank into the chair, resting her head in her hands with her elbows on Sandy's desk. "Why did she reach for the spray instead of her weapon?"

"You'll have to ask her," Sandy said, laying her hand on Laurel's back and gently rubbing. "She made a mistake. Fortunately, it's one she'll survive and learn from. You're supposed to be there to back her up, but you can't stop her from making mistakes from time to time.

You screwed up when you were a rookie, and no matter what you do, she's going to make mistakes, too."

"I should have noticed the plate." Laurel scrubbed her face with her hands.

"And that's a mistake you won't make again. Neither will she. You can't beat yourself up over this." Sandy squeezed her sister's shoulder. "Laurel, it's not like you to get this upset."

"You didn't see her." Laurel lowered her head and clenched her fists. "The blood...the damn blood. Can you imagine how bad it would have been if she hadn't been wearing her jacket?"

"But she was, and you said she's going to be fine." Sandy pulled Laurel to her feet. "Go home and get some sleep."

Laurel shook her head. "I've got to take care of Cheyenne and check to see how Nicole's doing." She turned and left without another word.

# Chapter Five

Jim pushed open the bedroom door and entered with a tray in his hands. "Dinner's ready."

"I can come downstairs to eat," Nicole said as she sat up. "It's only a few stitches. I'm going in tonight."

"Like hell you are. You said the doctor told you to take it easy for a couple of days. Not to strain your arm."

"Taking it easy doesn't mean staying home. It means, take it easy. It's bad enough I messed up and got injured. I'm not going to stay home for a few stitches."

"Laurel called twice while you were sleeping to see how you were."

"She did? Did she sound mad or concerned?"

Jim smiled. "Very concerned. I think she's got the hots for you, Nickie."

"She does not."

His smile grew wider. "Whatever you say."

"You're impossible." She looked at her bandaged left arm. "Do me a favor, and get me some plastic wrap so I can cover this when I take a bath. Hey, did anyone bring my car home?"

"No. You never bothered to give me your locker combination, so I couldn't tell them how to get the car keys." He settled the tray on her lap. "I bet Sergeant Sexy would give you a ride."

"You're not funny."

"Come on, eat your dinner that I slaved over a hot stove to make."

"Slaved over a hot stove?"

"Well, stood next to the microwave, same difference." He rubbed the back of his neck. "I wish you'd stay home tonight."

"I can't."

"I can call Mark and see—"

"Don't you dare," she said, sitting up even more. "I've got to go in tonight. Please don't fight me on this."

He scowled. "Fine but you'd better be more careful from now on."

"I will, I promise."

"I mean it, Nickie."

"Any mail?"

"Good mail and bad mail. Bad mail is bills. Good mail is our favorite presents from Aunt Edna."

Nicole smiled. "Checks. The gift that always fits."

"Fits for fifty bucks apiece."

"You opened my card?"

"I had to make sure you didn't get more than me," he said, pinching a french fry off her plate. "I signed mine and left it next to yours on the desk."

"I'll drop them off at the credit union tomorrow," she said. "We'll have to send her a thank you card."

"Yeah, thanks for not making us spend Christmas with her this year."

Nicole laughed and shook her head. "I'll write it, you sign it." She paused. "Did Laurel really sound concerned? You're sure she didn't sound mad?"

Jim chuckled. "Funny how our conversations keep going back to Sergeant Sexy. She didn't sound mad, I swear."

"Oh, good."

"Does she know you're planning to go to work tonight?"

"I'd assume so. I don't think she'd expect me to call out for this." She made a point of rotating her arm to show she had full range of motion. "I don't want her to think I'll stay home every time I get a little scrape."

"That's not a little scrape."

"I'm not staying home."

"So how are you getting to work?"

Nicole shrugged. "I'll call a cab."

"Ask Sergeant Sexy for a ride."

"Stop calling her that," she said, wagging her finger at him. She turned at the sound of the phone.

Jim waggled his eyebrows. "I bet it's for you."

Laurel pulled up and waited in the truck for several seconds before shutting off the engine. "I can do this," she said to herself, rhythmically gripping and releasing the steering wheel. "Just go in there, tell her I'm sorry she got hurt, and explain why." She told herself that again when she reached the door and once more when she rang the bell.

"Hi," Nicole answered the door and stepped back to let Laurel in. "Wind chill's really down there tonight, isn't it?"

"Good thing we'll be inside tonight," Laurel said, shutting the door behind her. "We have a stack of paperwork to do from last night, and we need to review the dashcam."

"Let me get my coat on, and I'll be ready."

Laurel took the jacket from Nicole. "Here, let me help you with that."

"Thanks."

Nicole barely shut the door when Laurel reached out and gripped her arm. "It's slippery out here. You should have Jim put some salt or sand down."

"Thanks, but I'm not feeling dizzy or anything. I'm sure I'll be all right."

Laurel almost let go, but a misstep on the bottom stair sent Nicole off-balance. It confirmed her initial resolve to help Nicole to the truck. "Easy, I've got you."

"Thanks."

She held onto Nicole's upper arm all the way to the truck. "It should only take a minute or so to warm it up in here again." Without thinking, she reached for the seat belt and secured Nicole in.

"You know, I don't think anyone's buckled me in since I was a little girl."

"Oh, well, um, your arm. I thought you might need help, that's all." Laurel shut the door and made her way to the driver's side. "Sandy can't stand my truck, but throw some weight in the back and some studded tires, and it's perfect for the winter." She started the engine. "Ah, see? Warm air already."

"It's okay. I'm not that cold."

Laurel drove several blocks before speaking. "You know if you wanted to take the night off, it could have been arranged."

"I'm fine. It's just a few stitches."

Laurel clenched her jaw. *A few stitches that never should have happened.*

"Laurel, Lt. Danko wants to see you," Debbie said as they entered the station.

Laurel nodded and turned to Nicole. "I'll meet you at roll call."

"Okay."

Laurel made her way to the lieutenant's office, expecting a good dressing down. She rapped on the open door frame. "You wanted to see me, Lieutenant?"

"Shut the door," he said, not bothering to rise from his seat. "Laurel, you want to explain this to me?" He pushed the request across the desk.

"I think John would make a better partner for Officer Burke."

"And this wouldn't have anything to do with her getting hurt last night, right?" He put his glasses on and held up a green paper. "You were pretty tough on yourself in your report."

"Just being accurate."

"I want to see Officer Burke's report when she's done with it."

"Arman, are you going to reassign her to John?"

"I talked to Mark about your request. You know he has a special interest in Miss Burke because of her brother."

"What did he say?" she asked, though she suspected she already knew his answer.

"No changes. He talked to her this morning, and we both watched the dashcam. It was a rookie mistake, Laurel. Nothing more. She moved into your line of fire and failed to withdraw to a safe distance when the suspect exited his vehicle." He handed her the report she had filed that morning. "I'll be waiting for both of your reports on the incident."

"Yes, sir," she said, understanding he was refusing the one she submitted. "Is there anything else?"

He laced his fingers together. "I've known you a long time. You're a good cop. Don't beat yourself up so much over this. Now go have a good shift, and make sure what happened last night never happens again."

Laurel sat redoing her report while Nicole worked on hers. Several times, she tried to find the words to explain how she felt, but they never came. Instead, an uncomfortable silence filled the room. "We'll be watching the dashcam once you're finished with that," she said without looking up. She heard Nicole's pen hit the desk.

"I'm sorry about last night."

"Why didn't you draw your weapon?" The question had bothered her all day.

"I didn't think deadly force was necessary."

"You didn't think? Nicole, he could have had a gun in his hand as easily as a blade." Laurel stood up. "You took a chance out there that I never want to see happen again, you understand?" Nicole nodded again. "I can appreciate that you don't want to use unnecessary force, but you carry a gun for a reason, and last night, that gun should have been in your hand and not in your holster."

"I know."

"I don't want to go to your funeral." She walked around the desk and looked down at the remorseful face. "You scared the hell out of me last night, you know that?"

"It won't happen again, Sergeant Waxman."

"You're right," Laurel said, leaning against the desk. "You have three days of light duty, and you're going to spend plenty of time reviewing traffic stop procedures. The number one rule is: If the suspect exits the vehicle, you back up and draw your weapon." She walked over to the window. "You don't stand there and allow yourself to become a target." She crossed her arms and stared out at the night sky for several moments before continuing. "There's something else. When I ran the plate, I didn't notice the dead bugs all over it. That's a giveaway that the plate had been on the front of a car, but with the snow and everything, well…I just should have noticed it. You'll see it on the dashcam."

"I should have seen it, too," Nicole said. "Guess I'm just lucky that my first major mistake didn't get me or you killed."

"We both made mistakes."

"Yeah, but I'll never forget it."

Laurel sat down in her chair, the unfinished report on the desk in front of her. "That's what matters. Finish your report."

"Laurel?"

"Yes?"

"I was wondering if you'd like some company when you go feed Cheyenne in the morning."

"I take it we're back to Laurel and not Sergeant Waxman?"

Nicole smiled and blushed slightly. "I'm sorry. I thought you were really mad at me for screwing up."

"I was worried, not mad. Well, maybe at myself, but not you. And you're always welcome to come to the stable with me. We'll make a horse woman out of you yet."

"So what's she got in there?" Sandy asked, keeping lookout from the doorway while Laurel searched through the refrigerator shelves.

"Hmm, let me see. Cherries, oranges, yogurt," she glanced over at Sandy, "but none of the kinds you like. Ooh, cherry cheesecake hidden on the bottom shelf."

"She'll know if we get into that. There's no chocolate?"

Laurel stood up and checked the freezer. "Nothing chocolate."

"What are you girls doing?" Elizabeth called from the family room.

"Nothing, Ma," they said in unison.

"I know better than that."

Laurel quickly shut the refrigerator, and they scurried over to the sink. Laurel picked up a glass just as her mother entered the kitchen. "I was just getting a glass of water."

"And your sister was just standing there making sure you did it right?" Elizabeth asked, giving both daughters a knowing look. "Stay out of the cheesecake. It's for dessert."

"I didn't touch it," Laurel said, leaning against the sink. "Sandy's having chocolate withdrawal."

"Snitch," Sandy said. "She's the one who put the glass on the piano without a coaster."

Laurel gave her older sister a dirty look. "Now who's the snitch?"

Their mother shook her head. "Both of you, stop it. Laurel, you know better. Just for that, you can sit at the kids' table tonight."

"Me? Why me?"

"Because there's not enough room at the table for everyone."

"So let Sandy sit with the kids."

"No way in hell," her older sister said. "I want to eat dinner, not wear it. You're the youngest adult, you sit with those brats."

"Watch your mouth, and don't call your cousin's children brats," Elizabeth said. "Now everyone has to sit somewhere. Laurel, you're at the kiddy table."

"I'm not sitting next to Grandma Goldman," Sandy said.

"She's going to sit wherever she wants, and if that's right next to you, then that's where she'll be."

"But, Ma, she smells like vapor rub. My eyes will be watering all through dinner if she sits next to me." Sandy turned to Laurel. "Wanna trade?"

"You? You sit with the kids?" Laurel put her hand over her heart. "Who are you, and what have you done with my sister? You sit with those 'evil little creatures' you can't stand?"

"I'll sit with the kids," Brian offered.

Elizabeth opened the oven to check the meat. "You will not. Laurel's sitting with the children, and you're going to be on your best behavior."

"It's not Dad who starts it," Laurel said. "Grandma hates him."

"She doesn't hate him," her mother said. "They just don't get along very well, that's all."

"Face it, Elizabeth," Brian said. "Your mother hates me. She has since the day she met me, and she will until the day she dies. She wanted you to marry a nice Jewish boy."

"I don't want to talk about this," Elizabeth said. "Mother will be here tonight, and I want her visit to be enjoyable."

Laurel moved close to Sandy. "So let Dad go stay in a hotel," she whispered in her sister's ear.

"Whatever you just said to your sister wasn't funny," Elizabeth said. "I swear you two act like little children when you're here."

"It's Laurel's fault," Sandy said, bumping her sister with her hip.

Smiling, Laurel returned the bump. "Is not."

"See? What do you need grandchildren for when you've got these two?" Brian asked innocently. His daughters looked at him in horror as the magic word was said.

"Motherhood is just what they need to start acting like grownups," Elizabeth said. "Let them each have a couple of children of their own and see."

"A couple?" Laurel asked, her eyes wide.

"Each?" Sandy added.

Foster & Miller

# Chapter Six

J im, it's not going to fit."

"Sure it will. Dad always got the tree in through the front door."

Nicole sighed and squeezed out from behind the tree. "It's just too big. You'll have to cut it down a bit."

"But Dad always got big trees."

"Jim, you were three feet tall. Everything looked big to you. There's no way we're getting this tree through that door unless you trim it."

"Maybe if Rob and I try to force it through."

"It's twelve degrees out here. Can we go inside and discuss this?"

"Come on, Nickie. We'll try one more time, and if we can't get it in, I'll borrow Rob's saw and trim it, okay?"

"Okay, but this is the last time. On three. One, two, three." They pushed as hard as they could, and with only a few broken branches, the seven-foot spruce finally made it through the doorway. "Okay, it's in. Shut the door."

Jim pulled off his gloves and hat, his blond hair sticking out in all different directions. "I told you it'd fit." He studied the tree. "I think we're gonna need more ornaments."

"It looks like you pulled every box out of the attic," Nicole said as she removed her outer garments. "We're going to be here all night doing this."

"It won't take that long if you'd stop bitching and start looking for the tree stand. Come on. This is supposed to be fun."

What her brother saw as fun, Nicole saw as revisiting the past and remembering Christmases when their parents were alive. "I've no idea which box it's in. Dad packed all this up the last Christmas."

"I opened those first three and found all the lights, but I didn't see the stand. Check the one on the chair."

She gave him a mock salute. "Yes, sir. Right away, sir."

Jim laughed. "Yeah, you know who's boss around here."

"Sure as hell isn't you," she said. "And that hideous thing you made in kindergarten is not going anywhere near the tree."

"Hey, it's better than that angel you made out of cotton balls and ice cream sticks."

"Fine, that'll stay in the box, too." Nicole opened the box, dusty from years of being untouched, and found a colorful array of holiday memories. Ornaments she and Jim had made in school were mixed with ceramic ones painted by their mother and glass ones nestled in their original boxes. "I forgot about this one," she said as she gingerly picked it up, her voice barely above a whisper. "Mom always put it near the top."

"You're not going to cry, are you?"

"And what if I did? I'm a girl, I'm allowed," she said, setting the ornament down. "I'm not going to cry. I just miss Mom and Dad, especially around the holidays." She reached down into the box and pulled out the green metal tree stand. "This really is a good idea, Jim." She set the stand on the floor and opened another box of ornaments. "It's about time we started having Christmas at home again."

"That's right," he said. "And I think the perfect way to do it is to get those animated reindeer for the front lawn."

"But you already have lighted things for the lawn," she said, absently stroking the candy cane ornament that her mother had knitted years before.

"Yeah, but haven't you seen those new ones? They have, like, a thousand lights or something, and they look like they're moving. Aw, come on, Nickie. They'll look great out there, especially if you let me get the sleigh, too."

"Sleigh?" She shook her head. "Oh, no. No sleigh."

"But you gotta have the sleigh if you're gonna have the reindeer. What good are nine reindeer without a sleigh?"

Nicole's eyes widened. "Nine? Nine?"

"Of course, nine. Rudolph and Dasher and Prancer and—"

"You're not putting nine reindeer with a thousand lights each on my front lawn. Absolutely not. No way, no how."

"It's my front lawn, too," he said. "And I want reindeer."

"One."

"One? Whoever heard of just one reindeer?"

"Anyone who pays an electric bill," she said. "One. Do you know how much those things cost?"

"Five."

"One."

"Four."

"One."

"Okay, okay…three. They're on sale right now."

Nicole sighed. "Two and that's my final offer."

"Two and I get the lighted candy cane for the window. It's only five ninety-nine." He picked up the tree. "You'll see." He wriggled the tree into the stand. "I'll make our house the best one on the block. Trust me."

"Yeah, trust you to make the electric bill higher than the car insurance." She knelt down and turned the pins to secure the tree. "More is not always better."

"It is when it comes to Christmas lights." He jumped when the phone rang, vaulting over the couch to grab the receiver before the second ring. "Hello? Oh, yeah, hold on." He turned and held the phone out to Nicole. "It's for you."

She grinned and took the phone. "Hello?"

"Hi. It's Laurel."

Nicole's smile grew wider. "Hi there."

"Are you busy tonight?"

"Busy? No." She turned her back to Jim. "What'd you have in mind?"

"Do you know how to bowl?"

"Bowl as in with a big heavy ball and pins?"

"That's the one."

"I played a couple of games with some friends back in high school, but I'm really no good at it."

"You know Candice Jackson? Redhead, about ten feet tall, works days?"

"I've seen her around the station."

"She broke her thumb. We need a fifth."

"We?"

"The Babes in Blue. It's my bowling team. We'll be at Shawn's Strike-O-Rama on Washington. Please say yes. It'll be fun."

"Sure, I'd love to go."

"Great. Practice time starts in half an hour."

"Doesn't leave me much time."

"I appreciate it, you know. I'll see you in a little bit."

"Okay. Bye."

"Bye."

Jim laughed and began singing, "Nickie's got a girlfriend, Nickie's got a girlfriend."

"Stop that, I do not," she said. "Her bowling team needs a substitute, and she asked me, that's all."

"Uh-huh. Nickie's got a girlfriend, Nickie's got a girlfriend."

"Cut it out. Just for that, you can decorate the tree yourself. I've got to get changed. Do me a favor? Start the car, and let it warm up for me."

"Oh, sure," he said, the mischievous glint still in his eyes. "Wouldn't want you to be cold on your way to see Sergeant Sexy."

Nicole bounded up the stairs. "Keep it up, and I'll cut the cords to all your lawn ornaments."

"Yeah, hurry up and change, so you can go see your girlfriend." He grabbed the house keys from the hook. "I'll see if Rob wants to go pick up some reindeer," he said in a voice too low for her to hear.

Nicole was surprised to see Laurel waiting just inside the double doors. "I thought you'd be practicing."

"Lanes don't open for another five minutes," Laurel said. "Glad you made it."

"I don't have shoes or anything."

"Don't worry, they have some lovely red and blue rentals available at the counter. You'll be the height of fashion." She held the door open and motioned for Nicole to go ahead. "After we get your shoes, I'll help you pick out a ball. You want a beer or anything?"

"I'll probably get a soda or something in a little while."

"Let me know when you're ready. I'll buy the first round."

Nicole smiled at the man behind the counter. "Eight and a half, please."

"Two fifty and you have to turn in your shoes."

Laurel nudged her. "That's so you don't take off with their snazzy shoes."

"You heard the lady," the man said, taking Nicole's sneakers and pushing them into the slot previously held by the rental shoes. "She's a cop. She oughta know."

Nicole smirked at Laurel. "You're a cop?"

"Hey, what can I say? Beats working in an office all day, and I get to carry a gun. Pay the man and let's go look at some balls."

A flirtatious comment about wanting to look at something else popped into Nicole's mind. Had the man waiting for payment not been there, she might have even had the courage to share the thought with a fellow lesbian. Instead, she handed over five dollars and waited for the change. She picked up the hideous-looking shoes and followed Laurel over to the rack of balls. "I've no idea which one to pick."

"Let's start you off with an eleven- or twelve-pound ball," Laurel said, bending to reach a ball on the bottom rack.

Nicole allowed herself a small smile as she checked out her friend's rear. "Sure. Whatever you say."

Laurel stood up and held out a black ball. "Here, try this one on for size."

Nicole accepted the ball, slipped her fingers in the holes, and nodded. "This works."

"Practice time begins now" came the announcement over the loudspeakers. "See Fran in lane eleven to get your raffle tickets."

"Come on, let's get down to our lanes."

"You do this every Tuesday?"

"Except next week because it's Christmas and the alley's closed," Laurel said. "Here we go."

Nicole looked toward where her friend was pointing and saw Debbie Singer waving at them. "You didn't tell me Sergeant Singer was going to be here," she whispered as they approached her.

"Hi, Nicole, I didn't know you were the one she called to sub," Debbie said, flashing a smile at Laurel. "Funny how you're the first one she thought of."

"You had a better suggestion?" Laurel asked. Nicole decided not to comment as the two other women quickly changed subjects and chatted while putting the balls on the return. She looked skeptically at the multi-colored bowling shoes and hoped there were no feet-eating germs waiting inside.

"Hello, Nicole."

It took a second for her to overcome her shock and acknowledge Laurel's sister Sandy standing in front of her. "Um, hi."

"Come on, Sandy, get your shoes on," Laurel said, opening her bright blue bowling bag and pulling out her own shoes. Nicole finished lacing hers and sat down next to Laurel.

"You didn't tell me the lieutenant was going be here, either," she whispered.

Laurel chuckled and pulled her laces tight. "Why? Does my sister make you nervous?"

"She is a lieutenant."

"Relax, she won't bite you." Laurel set her sneakers in her bag, then pushed the bag under the chairs. "Hey, Sandy, come here. Tell her there's no rank here, will ya?"

Sandy crossed her arms. "That depends on how good she bowls," she said, giving a stern look until she couldn't hold the laughter anymore. "We're off duty, Nicole. Here you can call me Sandy, but do it in the squad room, and I'll take your head off, deal?"

Nicole nodded. "Deal."

"Come on, let's get some practice rolls in," Laurel said to her. "And don't be so nervous," she added in a lower voice. "This is supposed to be fun, you know."

"I'm not very good at this," Nicole said.

"Candice is a 110 bowler. How much worse can you be? Come here. Take your ball and show me your form."

"You mean bowl?"

"Yes, show me how you bowl."

"No one's ever taught me. All I know is you run up to the line and throw the ball."

"You don't run, and you roll it more than you throw it, but you've got the general idea." Laurel put her fingers in a blue and white marbled ball. "Watch me." Nicole stood back as Laurel took her mark and rolled a strike. "See? Easy. Now you try it." To Nicole's surprise, her ball stayed on the lane and knocked down three pins. "Now try and pick up the spare," Laurel said. "Aim between the one and three pins, and you should be all right."

Nicole did as instructed, but the ball curved to the right, rolling into the gutter. "Maybe you should find someone else."

"Hmm, you have quite the hook there," Laurel said. "Do it again but this time, aim for the one pin." Nicole tried and was encouraged when six pins fell. "Let's hope you never end up having to pick up the seven with a hook like that."

Nicole nodded in agreement, her breath catching when she felt Laurel's hands on her arms.

"Try this. Your ball goes to the right, so start out left of the center to compensate." Nicole let herself be shifted to the left, losing herself in the rich timbre of Laurel's voice so close to her ear. "Try again."

Nicole's first instinct was to lean back against Laurel, but the more rational part of her brain kicked in and reminded her where she was. "Um, yeah. Okay."

"Hey, some of us would like to practice, too," Debbie said.

"And you could sure use it. Make no mistake about that," Laurel said. "One more time, Nicole. Remember, find a mark left of center and just relax."

Laurel stepped back, allowing Nicole to concentrate again. This time, the results were better. She grinned and gave Laurel a thumbs-up, then immediately rolled another gutter ball. "You sure you want me to sub?" She sat next to Laurel and watched the rest of the team take their practice rolls.

"I'm sure. You'll do better next time. Besides, we're here to have fun. If we win a game, that's a bonus."

Practice ended and the game began with Debbie picking up a seven-ten split. "Did you see that?" Debbie shouted as she jumped exuberantly into the air. "I've never picked up a seven-ten split!"

"It's about time you did," Laurel said, as she wiped her hands on a towel and picked up her ball. "You get enough practice at 'em." She stepped up to her mark and rolled a strike. Sauntering back from taking her turn, she said, "Go ahead, Sis."

"How come when she rolls a gutter ball, you tell her she'll do better next time, but if I happen to roll one, you laugh?" Sandy asked as she reached for her red and yellow spiral ball.

"Because it's more fun to pick on you." Laurel stepped down from the lane and slid into the empty seat next to Nicole. "I think having you here is bringing me luck."

"You don't look as if you need any luck."

Laurel shook her head. "Don't you believe it. We all need luck from time to time." She watched Sandy roll a strike and patted

Nicole's knee. "See, you're bringing the whole team luck. It's your turn. Remember to step left."

Nicole nodded and took her turn, knocking down five pins with her first ball and finishing in the gutter.

"Having fun?" Laurel asked, when Nicole sat back down beside her.

"Yeah, but I'm not doing very well."

"Sure you are. Look at it this way. Someone's got to keep those gutters from getting all dusty."

"Gee, thanks."

Laurel laughed and patted Nicole's knee again. "Just relax and have fun."

"It'd be easier if I didn't suck so badly."

"Hey, Rookie, you're up," Deb said.

Laurel smiled at Nicole. "Good luck."

Sandy took the seat vacated by the redhead. "Could she yell a little louder when you get a strike? I don't think they heard her over in Trenton."

"At least someone's rooting for me," Laurel said, her eyes never leaving Nicole. "And she's no louder than anyone else here."

"A blind person could tell you're interested in her," Sandy said. "You were practically in her lap a few minutes ago."

"We're just friends, Sandy. Good job, Nicole. Pick up the easy spare."

"You planning on having her keep subbing for Candice?"

"Sure, why not? Be at least six weeks before she'll be able to bowl again, if that."

"Why don't you just invite her to Sunday dinner?"

"You're not funny." Laurel picked up her ball. "My turn."

"Wow, I can't believe I made that spare," Nicole said as she sat down next to Sandy. "You're on a streak tonight. That was a pretty impressive split you picked up."

"Thanks." Sandy reached in her bag and pulled out a pack of gum and offered one to Nicole. Nicole declined and Sandy popped one in her mouth and put the pack back in her bag. "So you like bowling?"

"I never thought I did, but this really is fun," Nicole said. "I hope Officer Jackson feels better soon, though."

"Are you happy with the move from Hastings?"

"Oh, yeah, I love it here. It's nice not having to drive so far to work."

Sandy nodded. "It's nice to be able to work in your own area."

"I really lucked out when they assigned Laurel as my partner. I've learned more from her than I did in a year over there."

"Really?"

"Oh, yeah. She's a great partner," Nicole said, her eyes never leaving Laurel. "Great bowler, too. Look how easy she makes it seem."

"Uh-huh, great." Nicole missed Sandy's sarcasm.

"Talking about me?" Laurel said, standing closer to Nicole than her sister.

"I was just telling Lieu—, I mean Sandy, how wonderful you are as a partner."

Laurel smiled. "It's easy with you."

Sandy scowled and looked down at the scorecard. "You're up," she said to Nicole.

Laurel sat down. "What?"

"It's easy with you," her sister mimicked.

"So? It is. She's good with people and takes direction well. I forget sometimes that she's a rookie."

"She's a rookie and you're a sergeant. Try not to forget that. You don't need to be hauled up in front of Internal Affairs."

"Friends, Sandy. Friends. That's all it is. Why are you making such a big deal out of this?"

"Because I know you, Laurel. And I know it's more than a simple friendship to you."

"You're making a big deal of out nothing," she said. "You're up." She stood and met Nicole as she stepped off the lane. "You ready for that soda now?"

*Foster & Miller*

# Chapter Seven

Nicole entered the tack and feed shop, hoping to find the perfect gift for Laurel. All the typical gifts she had seen in the mall were either too impersonal or too intimate, and the experience had reminded her just how much she hated shopping during the holiday season.

A man behind the counter looked her way and smiled, displaying a wide gap in his front teeth. "May I help you?"

"Yes, please," she said to the clerk. "I'm trying to find a present for a friend."

"Does your friend walk on two legs or four?"

"Two, but she has a horse. I was thinking of something for her, but it would also be for Cheyenne. That's her horse."

"We have some very nice winter blankets," he said as he led her to a colorful display. "They're on sale."

Nicole blinked at the price and cleared her throat. "I was thinking of something a little less expensive."

"I know just the thing." He gestured toward a shelf on the far wall. "We have a grooming kit that's a great buy at only twenty-seven ninety-five. Even have them gift-boxed and ready to go. All you have to do is add the bow and gift tag." Nicole followed him over to the display as he continued to expound the features of the kit. "It has all the basics: body, face, and finishing brushes, curry comb, saddle soap, hoof pick, tack sponge, and a tail comb. Even has a carry tote to keep everything organized. It's the perfect gift for a horse owner."

"It does look handy," Nicole said, looking through the open display model. *Perfect. It's thoughtful, useful for Cheyenne, not too expensive, but it doesn't look cheap, and it doesn't imply anything.* "I'll take it."

"Is tonight ever going to end?" Nicole asked as she pulled into the parking lot of the Shop and Go Market.

"Rookies aren't allowed to bitch."

"Have you ever noticed how nuts people get around Christmas? I'll bet you anything he's got a broken arm."

"He's lucky she aimed for his arm and not his head with that skillet."

"I always thought that kind of thing only happened on TV." Nicole's eyes were drawn to the commotion inside the convenience store. "Here we go again."

"I want that nut arrested," a man behind the counter said as they entered the store. "She's going batshit and scaring away my customers."

"You heathen sinner," the gray-haired woman said. "You don't deserve to have any customers with the filth you sell."

Nicole walked over to the woman, who reminded her of Granny from the old TV show *The Beverly Hillbillies*. "What's the problem, ma'am?"

"I'll show you what the problem is," the woman said. "Sinners. The world is filling up with sinners, and just as God destroyed Sodom and Gomorrah for their evil ways, so he shall destroy this city of vileness." She reached for the display rack of condoms on the counter. "These are the poison." She held a package up in front of Nicole's face. "Do you know what this is?"

"Ma'am, what is your name?"

"Matilda Schuyler." She shook the red package. "Do you know what this is?"

"A package of condoms."

"It's the destruction of our world," the old woman said. "Right here, right next to the register where everyone can see it."

The clerk snatched the package out of her hand and placed it back on the rack. "They're big sellers."

"Sinner! Officer, you make him take them down and stop selling them."

"Miss Schuyler, it's legal to sell condoms."

The woman became more agitated. "He doesn't have to put them right here where I can see them."

Nicole glanced back at Laurel, who had her hand covering her mouth and a mischievous glint in her eyes. "Sergeant Waxman, do you want to handle this?"

"Oh, no, Officer Burke. I think you're doing just fine. Go right ahead."

Reluctantly, Nicole turned back to the woman. "Miss Schuyler, he can put the condoms wherever he wants to."

"No, he can't," she insisted. "I shouldn't be forced to see these." She snatched up the package of condoms again and shook it at Nicole. "I suppose you know all about these, don't you, young lady?"

Nicole heard a snort from behind her and fought to keep from laughing at the agitated woman. "Ma'am—"

"Immorality and sin on every corner as it is," the old woman continued. "Why don't you let him put those filthy magazines there, too?"

"Because the law says he has to keep those behind the counter," Nicole said. "Miss Schuyler, like it or not, he can put the condoms near the register. If you don't like it, maybe you should buy your groceries somewhere else."

"But this is the closest store."

"Then don't look at them."

"Sinners. Evil degenerate sinners."

"Don't you come back in here again, old lady," the clerk said.

"I'll starve to death before I ever enter this pit of evil again." Miss Schuyler stormed past Nicole and Laurel. "Be ready. The flood will come again to wipe out the sinful people and their sinful ways." She continued ranting as she left the store.

Nicole knew better than to look at Laurel; she was having enough trouble keeping a straight face as it was. "I'll need your information for the report," she said to the clerk.

Laurel got out of her truck just as Nicole pulled into the police lot. She leaned against the truck and waited for her, so they could walk into the station together. Once in the locker room, Nicole took off her coat and opened her locker. "What the...?"

Laurel glanced over to see what was wrong, then burst out laughing. "Jumping the fence, Officer Burke?"

Nicole crossed her arms. "Stop laughing."

"I didn't do it," Laurel said. "But you've got to admit it's funny."

"It's funny to you because someone didn't slip condoms through the vents of your locker." She pulled several red foil packets out and tossed them on the bench.

"I've a feeling this is only the beginning," Laurel said, checking her locker one last time before closing it. "I doubt the guys are going to stop with just sticking them in your locker."

"What do you mean?" Nicole asked. She found out when she went to inspect their patrol car. The backseat was filled with blown-up condoms of varying textures and colors. "Did you know they'd do this?"

Laurel chuckled. "No. You'd better get them cleaned out, so we can start patrol. Need a pin?"

"You get them."

"What's the matter, you never touched one before?"

Nicole felt the blush rising up her cheeks and turned away. "No comment."

*"Unit 105 and S109, Highway 17 eastbound before mile marker 51. Woman reports overturned vehicle."*

Laurel acknowledged the call while Nicole accelerated toward the accident. "I hope no one was hurt."

As Nicole drove under the Franklin overpass, she saw the overturned car resting against the guardrail. A young woman sat on the ground in front of it, her cell phone in her hand. "My mom's gonna kill me," she said as the officers approached. "Two days before Christmas and I total her car."

Nicole squatted down to talk to the young woman. "What's your name, miss?"

"Amanda Williams. I called my mom. She's on her way."

Nicole took the information from the teen, then put her in the patrol car to keep warm. She joined Laurel near the overturned vehicle. "She's not sure what happened but said something big came through her back window just before she lost control and flipped over."

Laurel knelt down and aimed her flashlight into the car. "I think your culprit is right there."

Nicole bent down to see. "Unless she usually rides with a concrete block in her backseat."

Laurel stood up and glanced back at the Franklin overpass. "It had to have come from up there."

Nicole shined her flashlight at the rear window and noted the gaping hole on the passenger side. "She's damn lucky it didn't hit the windshield."

"Do you want to ticket her for violating curfew?"

Nicole smiled at her. "You know I won't. The poor kid's been through enough tonight."

"You big softie," Laurel teased.

"Like I believe you'd give her one. You act big and bad, but you're a bigger softie than I am, Sergeant Waxman."

"Is that so, Officer Burke?"

"Yes, it is."

"Hmm, we'll see about that."

*Foster & Miller*

# Chapter Eight

*U* *nit 105, S109, fight in progress 609 Juniper Place. Several intoxicated females fighting in parking lot."*

"Of course, they are," Nicole said while Laurel answered the call. "What better way to start off Christmas Eve than to get drunk and have a fight?"

"Look on the bright side," Laurel said. "Maybe that cutie who gave you her number will be there again."

Laughing, Nicole shook her head. "No, thanks. She was only interested in the uniform. Besides, she's not my type." The Labrys came into sight. "There they are." Her eyes widened.

"There must be twenty of them," Laurel said as the cruiser came to a stop in front of the parking lot. Most of the women standing around the lot appeared to be spectators, but with a mob like this, fighting could quickly escalate. "Call for backup, just in case."

Nicole did as she was told, then steeled herself, grabbed her hat, and opened the door. "All right, break it up."

"Now look what you've done, you bitch."

"You started it, you dumb fuck."

"Enough," Nicole said, doing her best to look stern. She turned to the redhead who looked as though her nose was broken. "What's your name?"

"Rebecca Stone. I want to press charges against her."

"For what?" the other woman asked. "You can't prove nothing."

"Did I tell you enough?" Nicole asked. She pointed at the curb. "Go sit until I'm ready to talk to you."

"What the hell are you hassling me for? It's all her damn fault," the woman said as she walked away.

"I'm not the one who cheated with her lover's best friend," Rebecca shouted back. "You're both sluts."

"Maybe if you kept her happy, she wouldn't have come to me," a young blond with spiked hair said.

"You fucking bitch." The redhead lunged forward, getting past Nicole and landing a punch on the blonde before Nicole was able to subdue her. The blonde retaliated with a roundhouse kick that, unfortunately, landed squarely on Nicole's back.

"Bad move," Laurel said as she wrenched the spiky blonde's arm up behind her back. "You're under arrest for assaulting a police officer."

"Ah, come on. I didn't mean to kick the cop. She just got in my way."

"Doesn't matter if it was intentional or not. You assault a police officer, you go to jail."

Laurel watched Nicole grimace as she bent to step into her jeans. "You sure you're all right?"

Nicole put her hands on the small of her back and stretched. "Yeah, just a little sore." She sat on the bench to finish dressing. "I really wasn't expecting that. I thought everything had calmed down."

"Never underestimate the fury of a woman scorned."

"Especially one dumped on Christmas Eve." Nicole pulled a bright blue sweatshirt over her head, then ran her fingers through her hair to get the short red locks to fall right. "Do I have hat hair?"

"Just a little."

Ruffling her hair one more time, Nicole threw her gear into her bag and closed her locker. "I'm ready." Now that the shift was over, her mind went to the package hidden in the trunk of her car. She followed Laurel out, making small talk until they were in the parking lot. "Oh," she said, acting as if she just remembered. "There's something I want to show you." She began walking to her car. "It'll just take a sec."

"I hope so," Laurel said. "It's cold as hell out here."

Nicole had just reached her trunk when the back door of the station opened and the desk sergeant poked his head out. "Sergeant Waxman. I'm glad I caught you." Without a jacket, he shivered against the morning air. "Your mother just called. She said...." He looked down at the note in his hand. "Pick up a new set of menorah candles before you come over."

"All right, thanks, George." She turned back to Nicole. "So what did you want me to see?"

Nicole shifted from one foot to the other, unsure of what to do. "I didn't know...well..." She put the key in the lock and opened the trunk to reveal the brightly wrapped box with a silver bow. "I didn't know you were Jewish. I hope you're not offended."

Laurel laughed. "I'm not offended. My mother's side of the family is Jewish. Sandy, Tim, and I get lots of Christmas presents from Dad's side of the family."

"Happy Yom Kippur."

"Try Hanukkah."

The red in Nicole's cheeks was a combination of blushing and the bitter cold. "Happy Hanukkah."

"Thank you." Laurel rubbed her hands together. "So, do I get to open it now, or are you going to make me freeze to death first?"

Nicole laughed and gestured at the open trunk. "I hope you like it."

"I'm sure I will." Laurel lifted the box, then closed the trunk and set it on top. Breaking the tape that held the top flap closed, she lifted it to see inside.

"It's a grooming kit," Nicole said. "I guess it's a present for you and Cheyenne."

Laurel grinned as she examined the kit. "Looks like it has everything." She looked over at Nicole. "We'll use it today."

Nicole tucked her hands into the sleeves of her jacket to protect them from the cold.

Laurel picked up the box. "This really is very nice, Nicole. Thank you."

For a brief moment, Nicole debated trying to get a hug but decided against it, especially in the middle of the police station parking lot. "You're welcome. Can we get out of the cold now? I'm freezing."

Nicole went to Cheyenne while Laurel unlocked the tack shed. "Good morning, sweetie. How's my favorite horse today?"

"She's getting spoiled," Laurel said. "Must be all those extra carrots you sneak her when I'm not looking."

"But she likes them so much," Nicole said. "Don't you, sweetie?"

"Nicole?"

Surprised by the concerned tone in Laurel's voice, she turned to see her friend looking into the tack shed with a worried look on her face. "What's that?"

Nicole approached the tack shed, then smiled brightly when she saw the present sitting on top of a bale of hay. "Oh, Laurel."

"Merry Christmas. Open it."

"You didn't have to get me anything," Nicole said as she tried to carefully remove the gold paper.

"Just tear into it," Laurel said, crossing her arms and leaning against the doorway.

Nicole did the best she could, but in the end, the paper came off in several pieces, revealing a nondescript brown cardboard box. Inside, she found her present hidden amongst crumpled-up newspaper. "This is great," she said as she pulled out the bright green bowling bag. "Guess this means I'll have to buy myself a ball now."

"Look inside. There's more."

Nicole opened it to discover a pair of bowling shoes in her size, as well as a "Bowler's Crying Towel" littered with excuses for gutter balls and missed spares. She put the bag down and wrapped Laurel in a quick hug. "Thanks."

The brief hug sent a flush up Laurel's neck and into her face. She grabbed the rake and walked quickly to Cheyenne's stall. "You're welcome. Now let's get Cheyenne taken care of and go get something to eat. I'm starving."

"What are we gonna take down to make room for this?" Jim asked, proudly holding up his "Nicest Light Display" award from the local newspaper.

"How about your Little League picture?" Nicole asked, holding a purring Puddy on her lap.

"How about that one of me on my tricycle? I hate that one."

"I think it's cute," she said and realized that was probably why he hated it. "Fine. If you're going to climb up there, you can take that one of me on my yellow bike down, too."

"Yeah, you look ugly as hell in that one." He set his award on the couch and sat down next to the tree. "Can I open my presents now?"

"Open the green one first," she said. "Puddy, time for you to get down." She set the fat cat on the floor and leaned forward to take the small flat present Jim was holding out for her. "Thanks, Jim."

"I bet I know what this is," he said as he tore through the wrapping paper. "Yeah. Street Rumble Four. Excellent. Thanks, Nickie."

"You're welcome." Unlike her brother, Nicole was more delicate with the wrapping paper, sliding her fingernail under the seams and removing it in one piece to reveal a CD by one of her favorite artists. "I love Cheryl Wheeler."

"Just play it in your car and not in the house," he said. "I hate the way she sounds." He reached for a present the same size as the previous one. "Ooh, another game."

"I don't know why I bothered to wrap it."

"Me, either," he said, handing her another wrapped CD. "You can play that one in the house, but don't blast it."

"Excuse me, Mister It's-Not-Loud-Enough-Unless-The-Windows-Rattle?" She unwrapped the CD and smiled. "Heidi Batchelder. How'd you know she had a new one out?"

He grinned. "You got a flyer about a month ago. Gee, I must have forgotten to put that where you could find it."

"You sneak. Thank you. I can't wait to hear her new songs." She set the CD on top of the other one. "Let's open Uncle Terry's presents now."

"You know he got you another renewal for your Triple-A card. He always gives you that."

"Came in handy when I got that flat last spring," she said, glancing quickly at the card that came with the renewal. "What'd you get?"

Jim opened his card and smiled. "President Jackson. Two of them."

"Nice. Okay, your last present is here somewhere, but you have to find it." She grinned at the thought of how long it would take him. "I'll give you a hint. It's not upstairs, and it's not in the basement or garage."

Jim hopped to his feet. "Is it in the living room or kitchen?"

Her smile grew wider. "Yes."

He laughed. "Bitch."

"Okay. It's in the kitchen but no more clues."

"I'll find it," he said as he took off into the kitchen in search of his present.

"Can I open my last one now?" she asked, picking up the small box covered with red paper.

"No. Not until I find mine," he said as he opened and closed cupboard doors. "Is it big or little?"

"I'm not telling." She picked up her new CDs and read the song lists until she heard the silverware drawer open. "You're really hot."

He came back into the living room carrying the envelope she had hidden beneath the silverware tray. "Okay, open yours first."

"You first," she said, leaning forward in her seat and resting her elbows on her knees.

"No, you," he said. "Come on, I worked real hard to find it for you."

Never able to resist her brother's enthusiasm, Nicole smiled and opened the wrapping paper. She was surprised to see a flat jewelry box. She opened the lid and stared at the medallion resting in crushed blue velvet. "Jim, it's beautiful."

"It's Saint Sebastian, the patron saint of cops," he said. "I read about it on the Internet."

She blinked, then wiped at the moisture that blurred her vision. "It's very thoughtful." She stood up and moved next to him on the couch, opening her arms for a hug.

"I love you," he said before releasing her. "You can carry it in your pocket like a coin for good luck."

"I will," she promised. "Open yours."

He opened the envelope to find five twenty-dollar bills and two tickets to an upcoming concert by one of his favorite bands. "Oh, awesome."

"Thanks for driving me to the airport," Sandy said as Laurel negotiated the heavy traffic.

"That's me," Laurel said, "the family chauffeur."

"Don't forget to water my plants."

"I won't forget."

"The timers are set, and I called the newspaper. Make sure you pick up my messages, so the answering machine doesn't get filled up."

"I know what to do," Laurel said. "Are you sure you have everything?"

"Yes. This is going to be great. Six days with no beeper, no cell phone, just me and hundreds of single men trapped on a luxury liner."

Laurel laughed and changed lanes. "I don't know why you bothered to pack any clothes," she said. "I hope you packed some condoms, too."

"Funny thing about that," Sandy said. "I went into your desk the other day to get a pen to leave you a note, and there were several condoms in the drawer. Something you want to tell me?"

"The guys can't get over Condom Lady," Laurel said. "I hope you helped yourself."

"I did. I also bought a box just in case."

"Just one?"

Sandy nudged her shoulder. "I'm sure they sell them on the ship."

"I hope so. What are you going to do after the first night otherwise?"

Sandy stuck out her tongue. "You're just jealous because I'm going to get some and you're not."

"I don't want what you're going to get."

"No, you want what you can't have."

Laurel sighed and turned into the airport. "We're just friends, Sandy. Stop making more out of it than there is."

Laurel looked up from the report she was reading as the front door of the squad room slammed against the wall.

"It's gone!" Nicole shouted, her hair in disarray from the wind. "Gone! Someone stole it." She waved her hands in the air as other officers came running to see what the commotion was about. "Right out of the parking lot." Laurel dropped the report and rushed over to Nicole. "They stole my car. Thirty cars in that lot and they stole mine. Right out of the goddamn police parking lot."

"All right, calm down," Laurel said.

"Calm down? Someone stole my car!" Nicole shouted. "An eight-year-old car with over a hundred thousand miles." She ran her fingers through her hair. "Why would anyone want to steal it?"

Laurel led her over to one of the desk chairs and pulled it out. "Sit down, take a few deep breaths, and let's get the report started." She took the blank form being offered by one of the other officers. "The sooner we get this done, the sooner we can get the description out on the radio."

Nicole slumped into the chair next to the desk. "I can't believe someone stole my car."

Laurel was just finishing up the report when Debbie Singer walked over. "Well, I've good news and bad news for you," Debbie said.

"Uh-oh. I don't think I want to hear this." Nicole put her elbows on the desk and rested her head in her hands.

"The good news is they found your car." The red head popped up. "The bad news is whoever stole it ran into a telephone pole."

"They what?"

"Sorry, Nicole. It looks as if a couple of kids decided to get their kicks swiping a car from the police lot. A witness said he saw two kids running from the scene, but he couldn't give a good description of either one of them."

"How bad is my car?"

Debbie placed a hand on Nicole's shoulder. "Totaled."

"Thank goodness my car had airbags or the poor little darlings might have hurt themselves." Nicole slammed her fist down on the desk. "Damn, that pisses me off! They steal my car, wreck it, and run off without a scratch."

"Well, we don't know whether they were injured. We just know they were able to run away."

Nicole sighed. "Looks as if I'm going to need a ride to and from work until I can file a claim with the insurance company and replace my car." She glanced at Laurel. "You up for it?"

Laurel smiled. "No problem. I'm used to being a chauffeur."

"I'm telling ya, she just suddenly came into my lane and hit me," the irate man said, holding a bloody towel against his battered face. "She could have fucking killed me."

The woman in question sat in her car, her trembling hands gripping the steering wheel. "It's not my fault," she said, and Laurel could tell she was close to tears. "Something big came out of nowhere and hit the side of my car."

Nicole looked at Laurel, seeing the recognition on her face at the familiar tale. "Ma'am, where exactly were you when your car was hit?"

"Right there." The woman pointed. "I was just going under the bridge when it happened."

Laurel walked back to the overpass, shining her flashlight back and forth along the ditch that lined the side of the highway. There, in two pieces, she found a cinderblock.

"I hope this joker doesn't keep this up, or someone's gonna get killed."

Nicole nodded. "It boggles my mind that anyone would actually think tossing cinderblocks at cars is fun."

The sound of raised voices could be heard behind them, and Laurel hurried back to calm things down.

"...and I'm going to make sure they take your license away!"

Laurel stepped between them. "Okay, back off and calm down, sir. This accident was just that—an accident. Someone dropped a cinderblock off the overpass. When it hit her car, she swerved into yours. Neither of you is at fault. The fault lies with the person who dropped that block."

"Why would someone do that?"

"We don't know, sir, but it's not the first time it's happened."

"You mean someone's out there getting their jollies tossing cement blocks at people?"

"Afraid so."

The man shook his head. "Well, don't that just take the cake."

"Oh, my God, Laurel, you wouldn't believe it!" Sandy said as her sister finished putting the luggage in the back of the truck. "I didn't want to come home."

"You certainly look happy enough," Laurel said as she unlocked the doors.

"I never had so much fun."

"Did your fun have a name?"

Sandy fastened her seat belt. "Carlos." She smiled. "Tall, dark, and very well hung."

"Sandy. That's a little too much information."

"Oh, Laurel, I had the best time."

"Sounds like it. I don't see any tan."

"I didn't get out of my room much. Friday night, we were going at it so much, we ran out of condoms."

"Now that's definitely too much information. I'm surprised you're able to walk." Laurel put the truck in gear and backed out of the parking space. "Better hope you're not pregnant."

91

Sandy laughed. "Don't even joke about it. The last thing I need is a messy brat hanging on me."

Nicole watched Laurel rake the soiled straw into a pile. "I can't believe this was our last night riding together."

"We'll still be on the same shift," Laurel said. "I'll be just a radio call away."

"I know, but it won't be the same. I've learned so much from you."

"Hey, that doesn't have to end. We're just not riding together anymore."

Cheyenne nudged her shoulder, and Nicole gave her another carrot. "You're sure you don't mind driving me over to pick up the check from the insurance company?"

Laurel paused in her raking. "I don't mind. I've told you that before."

"I know, but I hate imposing on you."

"It's not an imposition, trust me."

"You can just drop me off if you want. It's a short walk to the credit union, and I can catch a bus from there to the car dealership."

"We'll go to the insurance company and the credit union, then car shopping." Laurel set the rake back in the tack shed and began shoveling the soiled straw into the wheelbarrow. "I'm wide awake, and it's too cold for you to be walking around out there."

"This one looks good," Nicole said, checking first the sticker price, then the interior. "It's in my price range and it looks clean."

"And ugly as hell."

Nicole laughed. "Okay then, what do I want?"

"What about that one?"

"A sports car? I'd never be able to afford the insurance. It more than doubled when Jim got his learner's permit. I can't imagine what it would be like if I bought a Z28."

"All right, the blue Mazda?"

Nicole shook her head. "I don't like hatchbacks."

Laurel looked around. "The gray Ford?" They walked over to the car in question. "Oh, forget it. Way too many miles."

Nicole peered inside. "It's also a lot older than I wanted to get."

"May I help you ladies?"

"Yes, I...Oscar?"

"Nickie? Nickie Burke?" He grinned. "I didn't recognize you with short hair. How are you?"

"I'm fine."

"Obviously, you're car shopping," he said. "How much are you looking to spend?"

"Not much."

"I have a very nice Audi over here. Low miles, nice red interior, ten thousand, but I'll take eighty-five hundred."

"I said not much," she said.

"But that's very reasonable considering the value you're getting. I'll get the keys, and you can drive it yourself and see how much you like it."

"Oscar, I really can't afford it."

"Well, you get what you pay for. I can show you cars that have a lower sticker price, but they're not going to be as perfect as the Audi is. Take it for a test drive, and I'm sure you'll see that it's exactly what you need."

"It doesn't make sense to look at a car that I know I'm not going to buy."

"Well..." He shook his head. "You don't want this one. Nickie, I'll tell you this and only because I like you. This car shouldn't even be on the lot. The engine is going and you see all the rust. Now the Audi is something you can feel good about owning."

"Let's go somewhere else," Laurel said, irritated by the salesman and his familiarity with Nicole. "I have a cousin who works at Presson Motors."

At the mention of a competitor, Oscar gave up the idea of selling his friend from high school the Audi. "There's no need to do that. I'm sure we can find something here to make you happy. Take a look at this beauty over here."

"If he shows you the vanity mirror, I'm going to hit him," Laurel whispered as they followed him.

Nicole laughed. "Behave. He's not that bad."

"He's a used car salesman. They're all bad. How do you know him, anyway?"

"High school. He helped me get an A in biology."

Laurel stopped walking. "He what?"

"He helped me…oh, not like that. We cut up frogs together in lab."

"Why didn't you say that in the first place?" Laurel asked as the quick jab of jealousy subsided. "He's still a shyster."

"Then it's a good thing I have you here to protect me."

Nicole got in her cruiser and made a few notes in her report before pulling out onto Walnut Avenue. She had just calmed down a domestic dispute and was grateful the combatants had settled down so quickly. What started as a verbal battle could have easily escalated into a physical brawl.

"*Unit 105.*"

She keyed the mike. "Unit 105."

"*Unit 105, proceed to 1067 Washington Street. Caller reports man with gun inside.*"

"Unit 105, 1067 Washington Street."

"*Unit 105, 1067 Washington Street. 2311.*"

Nicole pressed on the accelerator, watching the numbers as she sped up Washington Street. She came to a stop, double-checking the address against what she had written down. "Unit 105."

"*Unit 105.*"

"Confirm address on that man with a gun, please."

"*1067 Washington Street.*"

"Unit 105 clear." Nicole stepped out of her cruiser when Laurel pulled up.

"Wait for backup," Laurel said as she came to a stop.

Keeping her eyes on the museum, Nicole nodded. "I don't see anything."

"With any luck, whoever it is will be gone," Laurel said, crouching next to Nicole behind Nicole's cruiser. "Be careful."

Within minutes, three other cruisers pulled up alongside. "I guess that's our cue," the nervous rookie said.

Once inside, Nicole carefully worked her way through the wide, open areas. The security lighting was helpful, but she moved her flashlight back and forth to illuminate the shadowed areas in her search for the reported man with a gun.

"*Unit 72 to Unit 105.*"

Keeping her eye out for trouble, Nicole keyed her shoulder mike. "Unit 105."

*"I think I have something. West wing, over near the cannons."*

Feeling her heart race, Nicole took a deep breath and released it slowly. "Unit 105, clear." After a quick glance to see that Laurel had heard John's transmission and was heading in the same direction, she entered the museum's west wing. John and the other two officers who had reported to the scene were taking cover behind the series of cannons lining one side of the exhibit. Following the line of sight from their drawn weapons, she readied herself for a standoff...then blinked. "You're all evil people," she said, lowering her gun and staring at the eight-foot statue of a Revolutionary War hero complete with musket. The seasoned officers lowered their weapons as well and began chuckling at their successful joke. Hearing laughter behind her, she turned to see a very amused Laurel looking at her. "You knew about this, didn't you?"

"Consider it a rite of passage," Laurel said between laughs. "Did you want to read him his rights?"

*Foster & Miller*

# Chapter Nine

Nicole slowed when her headlights illuminated two mangled vehicles in the road ahead. One of the vehicles was flipped over, and she knew from the looks of it that if anyone was alive, he or she was in bad shape. She pulled over, turning on the flashing blue lights and aiming the spotlight at the cars blocking the road. "Unit 105."

*"Unit 105."*

"Request EMT unit and an ambulance at the intersection of Carter Road and Dogwood Street. Two vehicles, standby for occupants." Nicole stepped out of her car and carefully approached the accident. She gasped at the gruesome scene, knowing without getting any closer that the driver of the flipped red car was dead, his lifeless eyes staring at nothing. She tasted bile in her throat but fought to keep control as she made her way to the other vehicle. One look at the woman slumped in the driver's seat was all it took for her to lose control, barely making it to the side of the road before she vomited.

"Unit 105," she said into her shoulder mike. She stayed kneeling, unsure if she would lose control again.

*"Unit 105."*

Nicole paused before answering. "Request supervisor and coroner." She swallowed hard before continuing. "Two vehicles, one occupant each, both are DOA."

*"Clear 105. Request supervisor and coroner."*

Nicole put one hand on the ground and spit, trying to remove the horrid taste in her mouth as she heard the dispatcher contact other units to come to her location. She waited until she was sure her stomach was done roiling before making her way to the patrol car.

She used her coffee to rinse out her mouth as the sounds of sirens grew in the distance.

Laurel was the first on the scene and headed directly to the mangled cars. Nicole joined her, determined to keep her rebelling stomach under control this time. She watched Laurel circle the cars, her flashlight illuminating the grisly scene as she checked for open containers or any sign of drugs, both common causes of accidents.

Her flashlight stilled, and Nicole's eyes tracked to a cinderblock wedged between the woman in the upright car and the steering wheel. She was slumped over it, but the bloody edge of it was visible.

"Cinderblock boy strikes again." Laurel straightened and looked back at the train trestle that crossed the road about a hundred feet back. "Looks as if it came through the windshield right on top of her. She was probably dead before she hit the other vehicle."

They stepped away from the cars and Laurel noticed, for the first time, how pale Nicole was. "Is this your first fatality?"

Nicole nodded.

"First times are always the hardest. It'll get easier."

"I know." Nicole swallowed and took a few deep breaths, willing her queasy stomach to settle down. "I'll be okay."

Laurel carried both mugs to the table, setting one down in front of Nicole before sitting in the opposite chair. "How'd you sleep?"

Nicole nodded her thanks for the coffee. "Once I finally fell asleep, okay, I guess."

"You could have called and canceled dinner," Laurel said. "I would have understood."

"I know, but I wanted to see you before shift. Besides, I like your cooking." Nicole gave that smile that always warmed Laurel's heart. "It's nicer talking here than in our cars."

"Yes, it is."

"Shame we don't have time for a game of chess."

Laurel smiled. "You'll beat me one of these days."

"Don't you dare throw a game for me."

"I wouldn't dream of it," Laurel said. "You'll have to beat me fair and square." She put both hands around her mug. "So, no nightmares?"

"No. I kept seeing it when I closed my eyes, so I went downstairs and turned on the TV and fell asleep to it."

"It would have been all right to call."

"Why should you lose sleep just because I'm having a rough night?"

*Because I want to lose sleep when you're having a rough night. I want to be there for you.* "Hey, I'm your friend. Don't be afraid to call whenever you need me."

Nicole picked up her mug. "I thought about it," she said, looking over the rim. "It's so hard to believe someone would do those kinds of things to innocent people."

Laurel sipped her coffee. "I looked around, but I didn't see anyone out of the ordinary at the scene. It doesn't make sense that whoever would do this would just drop the block and run away."

"Think whoever it is will stop now that two people are dead?"

"Depends," Laurel said. "If it's kids who think it's fun to scare people, taking two lives might be enough to get them to stop, but it could just as easily be some nut who gets his thrills causing people to crash and die."

Laurel looked up from her paperwork and smiled at the red-haired woman who entered the squad room. "Feel like getting something to eat this morning before we go to the stable? I'm starving. I don't think I can wait till after."

Nicole patted her stomach. "I could go for something."

"Laurel," Debbie Singer called from the doorway. "Sandy called for you. She said she's on her way, and it was very important that you wait for her to get here."

"Did she say why?"

"No."

"Thanks."

"Guess breakfast is out," Nicole said.

"Sorry. I can't imagine what's so important."

"Do you want me to wait?"

"No. I've no idea how long this will take."

"I can go ahead and take care of Cheyenne for you. I don't mind."

Laurel looked at her watch. "You sure you don't mind?"

"Of course not."

Laurel scribbled down some numbers on a pad and handed it to Nicole. "Here's the combination to the padlock. I'll get up there as soon as I can."

"Okay. I won't give her too many carrots."

Laurel gave her a knowing smile. "Yes, you will."

"Yes, I will." Nicole motioned her closer, aware that they were not alone in the squad room. "Jim's friends are coming over tonight to work on a project."

"You have something in mind?"

"Open lanes at the Strike-O-Rama tonight. We could grab dinner in the lounge."

"My back's a bit stiff," Laurel said, leaning against the desk. "I think I pulled something."

"Oh. Well, we could just get dinner somewhere."

"How about you come over and I'll cook?"

"Sure," Nicole said, feeling very happy that she'd be spending the evening with Laurel instead of her brother and his rambunctious friends. "What time should I come over?"

"How about eight?"

"I'll be there."

Laurel had changed into her civilian clothes and was reading the latest issue of *Policewoman Monthly* when Sandy entered the squad room. "What's wrong?" she asked, immediately concerned by the pale look on her older sister's face.

"Everything," Sandy said, heading straight to her office. "I can't believe this is happening."

Laurel closed the door. "What's happening?"

"Oh, God, what am I going to do?"

Laurel reached out and grabbed her sister by the upper arms. "Calm down and tell me what's going on."

Sandy unzipped her purse and pulled out a piece of white plastic, the paper strip on the end a faint blue. "What am I going to do?"

Laurel's jaw dropped. "Are you serious?"

"Of course, I'm serious." Sandy dropped the pregnancy test on her desk. "I wouldn't joke about something like this." She shook her head. "I should have started my period eight days ago." She slumped into her chair. "This is just…oh, damn."

"It's just eight days. You could just be late."

"I'm never late."

Laurel leaned back against the desk. "What are you going to do?" she asked, half afraid of the answer.

"What can I do?" Sandy said, tears spilling down her cheeks. "You know I don't want kids."

"But you can't do that," Laurel said. "Can you?"

Sandy buried her face in her hands. "I don't know. I always thought so, but…damn it, I thought my chances were supposed to go down as I got older."

"It'll be all right. We'll figure it out." Laurel reached out and squeezed Sandy's shoulder. "The first thing you should do is find out for sure. Have you called a doctor?"

"No." She waved at her purse. "There's another test in there. I thought maybe I did it wrong the first time."

Laurel reached in and found a small glass tube, the liquid inside a clear blue. "I'd like to say congratulations, Sis." She sighed and put the tube back. "Whatever you decide to do, I'm right here for you."

"You can't tell Mom," Sandy said, looking up with tear-filled eyes. "Promise me you won't say anything to her, to anyone."

"Shh, I won't say a word, but this isn't something you can keep secret for very long." *Unless…* "Sandy, promise me something now? Promise you won't…you know, without talking to me first."

"Laurel? I…I had a lot of drinks those last couple of days on the cruise. Oh, God, what if the drinking caused birth defects?"

"And what if it didn't? Sandy, you can't freak out over something that may or may not have happened. The baby could be just fine. Have you talked to what's-his-name?"

Sandy reached for the tissues on her desk. "Carlos?" She shook her head and wiped her face. "I've no idea how to find him. I don't even know his last name." She began crying again. "I can't be a mother, Laurel. I can't. Of all the people to get pregnant."

"Come here." Laurel pulled her older sister into her arms. "You're not alone in this, Sis. I'm right here for you." She picked up Sandy's purse and put it over her shoulder. "Right now, I think you should take a personal day and go home."

"No, I should work. I can't let this interfere with my job."

"You can't work when you're upset like this. Come on, let me take you home. I'll stay with you."

"What am I going to do?" Sandy asked. "I don't want to be a mother."

Laurel glanced out her window and smiled when she saw Nicole's car pull into the parking area. By the time she had gotten to the stables, Nicole was already gone, and she didn't want to call for fear of waking her. She took a quick look at the stir-fry in the pan on the stove, then opened the front door just as Nicole came up the stairs. "Hi."

"Hi," Nicole said, unzipping her jacket. "Damn, it's cold out tonight."

"Only good thing is it's too cold to snow." Laurel held out her hand to take the jacket. "There's a fresh pot of coffee ready."

"Oh, thanks. I'd love a cup."

"Thanks for mucking Cheyenne's stall," Laurel said as she pulled down a blue mug from the hook. "I thought you were just going to feed her."

"I had a feeling you'd be a while, and I was there anyway, so…" Nicole shrugged and smiled. "It didn't take that long."

Laurel filled the mug and handed it to her. "Just the same, I appreciate it."

"I was happy to help." Nicole accepted the mug and blew on the steaming liquid before taking a sip. "How's Sandy?"

Laurel sighed and poured a cup of coffee for herself. "Not good."

"You want to talk about it?"

Turning off the flame on the stove, Laurel nodded. "I do, but I promised her I wouldn't say anything."

Nicole took their cups to the table. "I can keep a secret."

Laurel nodded, hoping it was true because she had no one else she could talk to about this. She slit the bag holding the rice, then poured equal amounts on two plates. "She's pregnant."

"That's great!"

Laurel shook her head and split the stir-fry over the plates. "Not for her. Maternal and Sandy are not two words that go together."

"She doesn't like children?"

"She didn't like kids when she was a kid," Laurel said. "She only tolerated me because I'm her sister, and she was old enough that she didn't spend much time with Tim." She brought the plates to the table and sat down. "It's hard, you know? I want to be happy and start buying baby things, but…" She poked her fork at her food. "She'll probably end up having an abortion." She looked at Nicole to see her reaction and found comfort and concern in those blue eyes. "I'd give anything to be a mother, and to her, it's the worst thing in the world."

"You'd make a good mother."

Her mouth full of food, Laurel nodded, then sipped her coffee to wash it down. "I'd like to think so. I know you would. You already have with your brother."

Nicole smiled and looked down at her plate. "Thank you."

"Do you want children of your own someday?" Laurel asked, trying to sound casual.

"Someday. Right now, I have to worry about getting Jim through college before I can think about children."

"Uncle Mark thinks he's a great kid."

"He's been so good to Jim," Nicole said. "Four kids of his own and he always finds time to spend with him."

"That's because the boys aren't interested in spending lots of quality time with their dad," Laurel said. She took another bite. "So, boys or girls?"

"Hmm?"

"Boys or girls? How many do you want of each?"

"I haven't really thought about it." Nicole smiled. "Okay, so I have. One of each would be nice."

"I want at least two girls. I think it's important to have a sister. Need more coffee?"

Nicole shook her head. "I still have half a cup. Two girls, no boys?"

"Of course, if I had a boy, I'd love him, but I'd really rather have girls."

"So why haven't you had children?"

Laurel swallowed before answering. "I don't want to be a single mom."

"So get a lover."

"Oh, sure. I'll just run right out and find Ms. Right. No problem." Laurel brought the coffee cup to her lips, surprised by how much was already gone. "I don't have them running up and giving me their numbers, you know."

Nicole smiled at the reminder. "That's never happened to me before, and I told you she's not my type." She pointed with her fork. "And I don't believe you don't get offers. You ever look around at the bowling alley? That short one on the Public Works team is always watching you."

"Karen? She does not."

"She sure as hell does." Nicole poked at her food with more force than necessary. "I'm surprised she doesn't need her bowling towel to wipe up the drool."

Laurel laughed, almost spewing the coffee she had been drinking. "She's never said anything to me about it."

"Maybe she's shy. Not everyone can just walk up to a handsome woman and ask her out."

"Handsome?" *She thinks I'm handsome?*

Nicole smiled and looked down at her plate. "Yeah, well...um, you're not exactly an ugly old hag with a wart on your nose."

Laurel laughed. "Thanks, I think."

"This is very good," Nicole said, pointing at her nearly empty plate with her fork. "You'll have to teach Jim how to make this."

"Jim? You don't do any cooking?"

"It's just the two of us, so usually we do the microwave dinners unless he's in the mood to make something. We don't have a dishwasher, so the fewer dirty dishes, the better." She scooped up a forkful of rice. "I can cook if I'm in the mood, though."

"I do microwave dinners a lot, too," Laurel said. "But that's only because I hate to cook for just myself."

"And you have a dishwasher," Nicole said.

"I wouldn't have rented this place without it. No dishpan hands for me." Draining her cup, Laurel stood up and reached for her empty plate. "I picked up an apple pie for dessert. It's in the box on the counter. You serve it up while I load these in the dishwasher."

"Yum. I love apple pie. You wouldn't happen to have any ice cream to go with it, would you?"

Laurel wiped her hands on a towel and opened the freezer. "As a matter of fact, I would." She heard the silverware drawer open. "Wait. You have to use silverware from that drawer." She pointed at the drawer next to the one Nicole had opened. "I try to keep a kosher house," she said by way of explanation.

"Explain that to me," Nicole said as she retrieved the proper spoon to dip the ice cream. "You have to have two sets of silverware?"

"It has to do with milk and meat," Laurel said, refilling her cup and adding sugar. "Jews don't mix the gift of an animal and the meat of the animal."

"So no cheeseburgers?"

Laurel chuckled at the aghast look on Nicole's face. "It's not the end of the world. I've never had bacon or pork chops, either." She followed the shocked redhead back to the table.

"I can't imagine not having pork chops," Nicole said.

"Good thing you're not Jewish then."

Nicole dished up two slices of pie and placed them in the microwave. "I take it you're not having ice cream on yours?"

Laurel shook her head. "I got it for you."

Nicole brought the plates to the table and scooped up a large dollop of ice cream on top of her pie. "I haven't had a good apple pie in ages. This really hits the spot."

They finished their dessert, and Laurel stood to clear the table. "Do you feel up for some chess?"

"Sure, let me help you clean up."

"I've got it," Laurel said. "You sit." She quickly cleaned up the kitchen table, glad that Nicole wanted to stay and play. "More coffee?"

"Sounds great," Nicole said. "I can get it myself."

Laurel put her cup on the table and went into the living room to get the game. "You want white or black?"

"Either one. So do you attend a Jewish church?"

"Temple, and not often, much to my mother's dismay." She returned to the kitchen. "Sandy's better about going than I am, and I think Tim goes when he gets a chance."

"How long has Tim been a Marine?"

"He joined right out of high school..." She thought about it for a second. "He's twenty-seven now, and he was nineteen when he joined, so eight years."

"It must be nice traveling to different countries."

"As a tourist, maybe. He sends Ma e-mails all the time, but he just tells her where he is. I don't think he spends much time sightseeing." She set up the board and gestured at Nicole to pick a color. "Want to see a picture?"

"Sure."

Foster & Miller

"I don't have photos all over the place like you do, but I do have one here." Standing up, she removed her wallet from her pocket and pulled out his picture. "This was back when he finished basic training."

"He looks like you," Nicole said, their fingers brushing against each other as the photo was passed.

"It's the haircuts," Laurel said.

"Your hair isn't that short."

"Close enough. I like it short."

"I think it looks nice the way you have it."

Laurel smiled at the compliment and began setting up her chess pieces. "Thanks, but I'm not the one the ladies at the Labrys are interested in. All eyes were on you when we've been there."

"That's because you hung back, and I was interviewing the combatants. It was a circus, and I was in the center ring." Nicole put her pawns on the board. "And they'd have to be blind not to notice you."

"You think so?"

"I know so," Nicole said. "You go first."

*Is she flirting with me or just being nice?* "You ever go there? The Labrys?"

"I've been a few times. I hate when you move that pawn. You?"

"You hate it because it allows my bishop out," Laurel said. "In my younger and wilder days, I went there, but it wasn't the meat rack that it is now. You sure you want to move that knight?"

"Like I have a choice. I'm not letting you fool me again and get my queen." She held her finger on top of the knight for several seconds while looking carefully at the board. "Is that where you met Theresa?"

"Actually, I stopped her for speeding. Ran into her again in the supermarket and things just went from there." Laurel moved a pawn, smiling at how quickly Nicole jumped to take it with her knight.

"Do you miss her?"

Laurel hesitated, then used her pawn to take Nicole's knight. "I don't miss Theresa as much as I miss coming home to someone."

"You didn't have to do that," Nicole said, moving her other knight into play. "I've lost already, haven't I?"

"Not quite."

"Did you two live here?"

106

"Good move. No, I moved in here about a year and a half ago. It's small, but I don't need much."

"It's not small, it's cozy. I like it. You know what a pain it is to keep a three-bedroom house clean?" She moved a pawn. "Go ahead, take it. I know you want to."

Laurel laughed and took a different pawn with her bishop. "I'd love a nice big house with some land, maybe a creek or pond."

"Cheyenne would love that," Nicole said. "Don't you dare take my queen."

"How can I resist when you put it right out there for me?" Laurel used her knight to take her opponent's most powerful piece. "Not just Cheyenne. I'd love to breed and raise horses full time."

"Your children would be thrilled. Don't all little kids want their own horse?"

"I did," Laurel said. "And Dad said what most parents say: No way in hell."

"I knew better than to ask for one," Nicole said, doing her best to keep Laurel from winning too quickly as they played game after game and chatted on with no regard for the time.

Laurel leaned against the doorway. "Hey."

Sandy turned around, showing dark circles that spoke of a long night with little sleep. "What are you doing here on your day off?"

"I called your house, but you'd already left," Laurel said as she entered her sister's office.

"I don't want to talk about it here," Sandy said, taking off her coat and hanging it on the rack.

"You coming tonight?"

"I think so." Sandy dropped her purse on the desk. "I didn't get much sleep last night."

"You should have called. I was up."

"I know you were. I went for a drive around two, and your lights were on."

Laurel was surprised. "Why didn't you stop?"

Sandy crossed her arms. "What was Nicole Burke's car doing parked next to yours?"

"She came over for dinner, and we played chess and talked."

"At two in the morning?"

"At two in the morning," Laurel said. "You should have come in or called if you needed to talk."

"I wish you didn't spend so much time with her. I just have this feeling that you're going to get hurt."

"How many times do I have to tell you that we're just friends?" Laurel pulled the roller shade down. "Did you make a decision?"

"I told you I didn't want to talk about it here." Sandy sighed and sat in her chair. "I'm going to call this morning for an appointment."

"With an obstetrician?"

"With the clinic."

The words hung in the air for several seconds before Laurel spoke. "You have other options, you know."

"I don't want to be a mother."

Laurel put her hands on the desk and leaned toward her sister. "You don't have to have an abortion. There are thousands of people out there who would love the chance to be parents to this child."

Sandy looked away. "I've made my decision."

"It's wrong. It may be legal, but it's wrong." Laurel turned away from her older sister. "Think about this, please. It's not like you have to do it right away."

"I do," Sandy said. "Please, Laurel, don't make this harder on me."

"It should be hard. This isn't returning a sweater that doesn't fit. You're talking about your baby."

"I know that. My mind is made up."

"Fine." Laurel stood and walked to the door. "I'm going home. Leave me a note or call me to let me know when your appointment is."

"Why?"

Laurel rested her hand on the door handle and looked back at her sister. "Because even if I don't agree with what you're going to do, I love you too much to let you go through something like that alone." She opened the door. "I'll see you tonight, and, Sandy? Please think about this some more."

# Chapter Ten

I told you she has the hots for you," Nicole said, the sounds of falling pins and balls hitting the lane keeping her words from reaching anyone other than the one she intended.

Laurel glanced quickly at the short blonde from the Public Works team, then back to the redhead she found far more interesting. "She likes the way I bowl. Besides, she's not my type."

"And what is your type?"

*You.* "What's yours?"

Nicole smiled. "I asked you first."

"Laurel, you're holding us up," Sandy said from her chair several feet away.

"Saved by the bowling ball." Laurel gave Nicole a wink before stepping up onto the lane. Distracted by her thoughts, she missed the headpin on the first roll, then settled down and picked up the spare. "There goes my chance for a 180 game," she said as she returned to Nicole's side.

"I'd be happy to get 120," Nicole said. "So?"

Laurel smiled, pretending to watch her sister bowl, though she could see Nicole with her peripheral vision. "What do you think my type is?"

"Oh, no, you don't."

"It was worth a shot. You're up."

"Saved by the bowling ball again," Nicole said. "Nice strike, Sandy."

"Yeah, nice strike," Laurel said as her sister approached.

"Like I believe you were watching me," Sandy said. "I could have thrown two gutter balls for all you knew."

"Nicole and I were talking. You don't always watch me take my turns."

"I'm not the one you want watching you, and don't give me that 'just friends' crap." Sandy leaned over to retrieve her glass from the counter behind the chairs.

"I don't want to talk about it," Laurel said. "What are you drinking?"

Sandy wiggled the glass in her hand. "Club soda and cranberry juice, Mother Hen. I didn't want to listen to you if I had a beer."

"Does this mean you've changed your mind?"

"It means I don't want to be nagged tonight. It'll all be over by this time Thursday, and I don't want to talk about it anymore."

Laurel shook her head. "I'm not trying to nag you," she said, knowing the subject was closed when Nicole approached. "You almost had that spare."

"I wish I didn't hook so much," Nicole said, looking from Laurel to Sandy and back again. "Um, I think I'll go get a drink."

"You're not interrupting anything," Sandy said, setting her drink on the counter. "Excuse me." She walked off toward the ladies room.

"You okay?" Nicole asked quietly.

Laurel sighed and reached for her drink. "I will be."

"Do you want to talk about it?"

"Not now."

"If you need to…"

Feeling the tender touch on her forearm, Laurel looked at Nicole and smiled. "I know. That goes both ways."

"Are you going to say anything to me?" Sandy asked.

Laurel continued to look straight ahead as she drove through the business district. "What do you want me to say?"

"I don't know, but I hate this silent treatment."

Slowing for a traffic light, Laurel sighed and flexed her hands on the steering wheel. "You know how I feel about this."

"I told you I could drive myself."

"And I told you that I wouldn't let you go through this alone."

"I can't believe I'm actually doing this."

"It's not too late to change your mind."

Sandy didn't answer and silence reigned in the car until Laurel turned into the family planning clinic's parking lot. "Please think about this, Sandy."

"That's all I've been doing," Sandy said, a tear spilling down her cheek. "I've always said that it was okay for others but not for me." She sniffled and pulled a tissue out of her purse. "Of course, I never thought I'd get pregnant."

Laurel unbuckled the seat belt and twisted, so her back was against the driver's door. "Put the baby up for adoption."

"And how do I explain that to Mom? She'd never forgive me."

"She'd forgive you for that before ever forgiving an abortion. Our HMO covers counselors. You could go talk to one. I'll even go with you if you want." She reached out and rubbed her sister's shoulder. "Please think about this some more because once it's done, there's no going back. Look how upset you are now. How can you make a decision like this without being totally sure?" She sighed and removed the key from the ignition. "Okay, I won't push anymore. Let's go."

Sandy looked at the building through tear-filled eyes. "I...I can't do it." She buried her face in her hands. "I can't, Laurel. Oh, God. What am I going to do?"

"Come here," Laurel said, opening her arms to her older sister. "It'll be all right, Sis. We'll figure it out together."

Nicole approached the enclosed porch and saw a woman standing in the doorway. She noticed that the woman's right eye was swollen shut and blood trickled from her nose. "He's in there," the woman said.

"Does he have any weapons?"

"A knife."

Nicole thought the woman's action odd but told her to go wait at the far end of the porch where another officer would get her information.

"I'll take point," Officer John Decker said, his service weapon in his right hand. He led the way down the hallway, stopping at the nearly closed door. "Andre, it's the police. Put the knife down and come out with your hands up." Nicole felt her heart pounding in her chest as she waited for the suspect to come out. When several seconds passed with no sounds coming from the room, John motioned for her to take position on the right side of the doorway while he took the left side. "Andre, don't make me come in there," John said. Still no response from behind the door. "Ready?" he quietly asked her.

Nicole nodded, wishing her hand wasn't sweating so much around the grip of her Glock. John kicked the door open and crouched, both officers aiming their weapons at the darkened silhouette on the bed. Keeping her gun on the suspect, Nicole reached up with her right hand and flipped the light switch. "Oh, damn." Nicole felt her stomach churn at the bloody sight. "I'll go cuff her and call for homicide," she said, wanting more than anything to get away from the man lying on his back with dozens of stab wounds and a knife sticking out of his chest.

Nicole stepped outside and radioed for the homicide squad, then motioned to the officer watching the woman. "He's dead," she said when he reached her.

The officer nodded. "She said she stabbed him."

"About twenty times at least," Nicole said. A patrol car pulled up, and she almost smiled when she saw Laurel step out. "I'll go tell Sarge what's going on."

"Okay, I'll cuff her," the officer said.

Nicole met Laurel halfway between the curb and the porch. "And you thought it'd be a boring night."

"Bad?"

"Looks like she lost control and stabbed him to death. There's blood everywhere in there."

"Find the weapon?"

Nicole nodded. "It's still in his chest." She crossed her arms as a cold wind blew past. "So much for leftover spaghetti for dinner break."

"I have a corned beef sandwich," Laurel said. "We can share."

"I'll be fine but thanks," Nicole said. "I don't think I could eat anyway."

"So what are you going to do on break?"

Nicole shrugged. "Go sit at a speed trap, I guess."

"You want company?"

After a quick glance to make extra sure no one was within earshot, Nicole tapped her finger to her chin and looked upward. "Let's see. Sit at a speed trap by myself or spend the time with you. What a hard decision."

"It's a good thing you're cute," Laurel said. "Now let's get the crime scene tape up."

Nicole smiled. *She thinks I'm cute.*

"Please don't do anything to tick Mom off," Sandy said. "I don't think I could take her talking about grandchildren right now."

"Why don't you tell her that you're not feeling well and go home?" Laurel asked.

"What am I going to do? Pretend to be sick and hide from her until after it's born?"

"Then tell her."

Sandy shook her head. "No. I can't tell Mom yet."

"Tell me what?" Elizabeth asked as she entered the kitchen.

"Uh, that I'm thinking of remodeling my kitchen," Sandy said. "I can't decide between maple and oak cabinets."

"You have a perfectly nice kitchen." Elizabeth made her way to the oven and peeked inside at the roast. "And besides, why wouldn't you want me to know you're thinking of remodeling your kitchen? You two are up to something."

"We're just talking," Laurel said.

"Right, just talking," Sandy said.

Elizabeth looked at her daughters. "I'm not sure if I should worry more when the two of you are at each other's throats or when you're conspiring together." She wagged her finger at Sandy. "And don't think for a minute I believe one word about remodeling your kitchen. Your sister is the last person you'd ask for advice about that."

"Ma, I'm not totally useless when it comes to decorating," Laurel said.

Elizabeth lifted the lid off the pot on the stove and stirred the contents with a wooden spoon. "And just who was it that wanted to put lavender curtains up in a room with green carpeting?"

"I think I'll go see what Dad's doing," Laurel said.

"I have to talk to Uncle Mark about something," Sandy said.

"I don't know what you two are up to, but I'll find out soon enough," their mother said as the sisters left the kitchen. "Neither of you could keep a secret from me for long."

"She's right, you know," Laurel said when they slipped into the privacy of Sandy's old bedroom. "You can only keep this from her for so long."

"I just can't figure out what to say to her," Sandy said, flopping back on her bed. "What am I going to do?" She sighed and raked her fingers through her hair, then let her arms fall limply to the sides. "Hey, Mom, guess what? I'm pregnant but you're still not getting a grandchild to spoil. If she didn't have a stroke, she'd kill me."

"What about me?" Laurel sat next to her. "I could take the baby."

"And have it grow up knowing who I am and that I gave it away?" She stared up at the ceiling. "I'll make arrangements with an adoption agency. It's better that way."

Nicole slowed down for the traffic light, appreciating a sunny day with temperatures closing on the mid-forties. Looking around, she saw that many people were enjoying the unusually warm day in early February, visiting the downtown stores and walking on sidewalks free of snow. As she waited for the light to change, she noticed a small woman sitting on the bench at the bus stop. "Hey." Pressing the button to lower the passenger window, Nicole leaned over and called to the woman. "Miss Schultz?" The car behind her beeped, drawing her attention to the fact the light had turned green. Surprised to see her old high school English teacher, she turned the corner and pulled into the first available spot. She stepped out of the car, smiling when she saw the woman stand up and look at her. "It is you," she said.

"And you're...now don't tell me."

Nicole smiled. "I took honors English, creative writing, and women in literature from you."

"Begins with a B. It's not Burton."

"Burke."

"Burke." The gray-haired woman smiled. "Nickie Burke."

Nicole nodded. "So how are you?"

Miss Schultz waved her hand, the fingers twisted by arthritis. "Not so good," she said. "The body gets old even when the mind stays young."

"Are you waiting for the bus? I'd be happy to give you a ride."

"You're sure it wouldn't be any trouble?"

"No trouble at all. It'll give us a chance to catch up." Nicole guided her to the car and helped get her seat belt fastened. "It's so good to see you again," she said before making her way around the car. "I haven't seen you since...well, I was going to say my graduation, but you were at the funeral, weren't you?"

Miss Schultz nodded. "That was so sad."

Nicole started the engine. "So where are you headed?"

"Ten Sequoia Avenue."

"That's over near the city line, isn't it?"

"Yes. It's good to see you, too, Nickie. What have you been up to?"

"I'm a police officer now."

"You are?"

Nicole was surprised by the excitement in Miss Schultz's voice. "Yeah."

"Then perhaps you can help me."

"Sure, what can I do for you?"

"My friend Cheryl has disappeared. I think my landlady did something to her."

"What makes you think that?" Nicole asked, glancing over to see the serious look on the wrinkled face.

"She lived across the hall from me. One night, she was there, and the next day, she was gone." Miss Schultz turned to Nicole, her eyes glistening with unshed tears. "I know she didn't move away like Liza says."

"Who's Liza?"

"She's the one who owns the boarding house. I may be old, but I'm not crazy. Liza did something to Cheryl, I just know it."

Nicole turned onto Highway 4, planning on bypassing the suburban streets on her way to the outskirts of the city. "What makes you sure she didn't move?"

"She didn't. I know she didn't. She'd have told me. We were...close. We had tickets to the Christmas extravaganza on Saturday, and she disappeared Thursday night."

"So she's been gone two months?"

Miss Schultz nodded. "At first, I thought Liza had kicked Cheryl out, and she didn't have any way to reach me by phone, but I waited and waited, and I haven't heard a word from her."

"Did you report it to the police?"

The elderly woman nodded. "I spoke with a Detective Briggs, but when I went back and asked him about it, he told me that she moved just like Liza said." She reached out and touched Nicole's arm. "Please, Nickie. Cheryl wouldn't have just left me. Something happened to her."

Rumors heard in high school sprang forth from Nicole's memory. "Miss Schultz, I don't want to offend you, but were you and Cheryl...?" The sobs she heard answered the question. Popping open the console between the front seats, Nicole pulled out several tissues from a travel pack and handed them to her former teacher. "I came out when I was nineteen," she said. "No wonder you were my favorite teacher. I thought you might be, but I wasn't sure."

Miss Schultz dabbed her eyes. "You have to help me find her."

"I'm not sure what I can do if a detective has already investigated it, but I'll try." Nicole turned onto Sequoia Avenue, absently noting she was in the 400 block. "If you open the glove compartment, you'll find a notepad and pen. Write down all the information you know about Cheryl. Her age, description, the names of any family she might have that you know about, anything that might be helpful."

"My penmanship isn't what it used to be," Miss Schultz said as she opened the glove compartment.

"That's okay. I'm sure I'll be able to read it. How long have you lived there?"

"Just over a year."

"Why did you move there?"

The elderly woman sniffed. "The man who owned the house I was renting died, and his son sold it. I had to move, and I just couldn't afford what a nice place costs these days. Liza's boarding house seemed like the perfect solution when I moved in."

"How long did Cheryl live there?"

"She moved in just after I did."

"I understand she wouldn't leave you, but what makes you think your landlady did it?"

"I'm always a light sleeper, but that night, I was so very tired after dinner that I had to go to bed, and I didn't wake up until the next afternoon, and when I did, Liza said Cheryl had just moved out, and she didn't know where she had gone." She reached out and touched Nicole's arm again. "Please believe me. I'm so very worried about her."

"What can you tell me about Liza?"

"Everyone likes her. She makes you feel that she's your friend, but she's very controlling."

"Controlling how?"

"She won't let anyone get the mail, ever. She's the only one who has the key to the mailbox. I received a letter from the Teacher's Retirement, and it looked wrinkled, as though it had been steamed open, then sealed back up."

"Do you still have that letter?"

"No."

"What else?"

"I think she's been in my room when I wasn't there. I've found things not quite the same way I left them. She said she hadn't, but she had this look in her eyes...Nickie, believe me when I tell you that I was scared. I know that woman is capable of taking a life, I can feel it."

"Has she ever threatened you or anyone else that you know of?"

"One night, just before Nelson Bing moved out, I heard her arguing with him downstairs, but I couldn't tell what they were saying. I can't hear much when the door's closed." Miss Schultz wiped her face one more time and put the crumpled tissue into her purse. "He moved out a few days later. Oh, do you think she might have done something to him, too? I hadn't thought of it before, but I went to sleep early that night, too."

"I really don't know." Nicole pulled the car over to the curb in front of a large two-story home, the back yard blocked from view by a high stockade fence with a locked gate.

"Oh, dear, she's looking out the window."

Nicole looked to see a curtain pulled back slightly, though she couldn't see anyone peering out. "Miss Schultz, do you think she'll hurt you?"

"I don't know. She doesn't like people coming over. Will you come back to see me?"

"Of course. Do you have a phone?"

"No. Liza has one, but she keeps it locked in her room. Sheila Hadley had a gall bladder attack, and we couldn't call for an ambulance until Liza came home." She looked out the window again. "I'd better go."

"Is there a time when she's not home that I can come back to see you?"

"She usually goes shopping on Fridays. She leaves around noon."

"Okay, I'll come back then," Nicole said. "Are you sure I can't put you up somewhere, so you don't have to go back there? I really don't mind at all."

"No, dear. I need to stay here and watch Liza. That's the only way I can hope to prove what she did to Cheryl."

Nicole hesitated, then scribbled her number on a piece of paper and handed it to her friend. "Call me if anything suspicious happens, and I'll see you on Friday."

Miss Schultz took the paper and slipped it in her purse.

"You be careful now," Nicole said. "It was really nice to see you again."

"Thank you. It's nice to see you, too, and I do appreciate what you're doing for me." Miss Schultz reached for the door handle.

"Oh, here, let me help you," Nicole said, reaching for her own handle.

"Oh, no, I can get it," the elderly woman said. "I'll see you Friday?"

"I promise."


"Are you sure this isn't a case of a lover's quarrel?" Laurel asked, tugging the laces of her bowling shoes tight and sitting up.

"I don't know," Nicole said. "Miss Schultz said she and Cheryl had tickets to go to the Christmas Extravaganza downtown. I wouldn't make plans to go somewhere with someone I was fighting with."

"You would if you wanted her to think everything was fine," Laurel said. "If you were planning to leave and didn't want any kind of scene." She shrugged. "Or if the tickets were purchased before they quarreled."

"She didn't give any indication they were having any spats," Nicole said, tucking her sneakers in her bag. "I wanted to ask Detective Briggs what he found out, but he won't be in until Thursday."

"Have you ever met Louis Briggs?" Laurel asked.

"No."

"Uh-huh. Well, for starters, he's married, but he doesn't act like it. He offered to..." Laurel made quote marks with her fingers. "...help me see what a real man can offer."

Sandy joined them and heard the tail end of their conversation. "Briggs is harmless once you put him in his place."

"He can be a bit intimidating, though," Laurel added. "I'll talk to him for you if you'd like."

"Do you hold her hand when she interviews witnesses, too?" Sandy asked, giving her sister a dirty look before walking away.

"Excuse me, Nicole," Laurel said. "I'll be right back."

Laurel hit the ladies room door with both hands. "What the hell was that all about?"

Sandy stood in the middle of the bathroom, hands on her hips. "She's supposed to be a cop. If she can't handle talking to Louis, then she shouldn't be on the force."

Laurel moved until she was within arm's length of her sister. "What do you have against her?"

"I don't have anything against her. What I'm against is the idea that you're going to do something that could jeopardize your career. She's a rookie and you're a sergeant."

"I'm not allowed to have a friend?"

Sandy pushed off the counter and began pacing. "You may be fooling yourself into believing you're only interested in her as a friend, but you're not fooling me." She scratched her head. "Maybe you don't see it because you're so attracted to her. Tell me one friend you've ever had who you jumped up and bought drinks for or took with you every day to the stables to see your horse or stayed up till the wee hours playing chess or..." She stopped when the bathroom door opened and someone came in. They remained quiet until the woman left.

"All right," Laurel said, crossing her arms. "I get your point. And for the record, she doesn't go with me to see Cheyenne every day, just on the mornings after we've finished our shifts."

"I don't dislike her," Sandy said. "I just worry you're so wrapped up in her that if this blows up in your face, you're going to be hurt even worse than with Theresa." She stopped pacing and put her hands on the counter. "You never invited Theresa to join the bowling team." She sighed. "Laurel, I'm sorry if I was rude out there. I didn't mean to, I just..."

Laurel softened her stance. "I know, Sis. I know you have a lot on your mind right now, and you're worried about me, too." She moved closer and rested her hand on her sister's shoulder. "You don't have to worry about me. I admit I'm attracted to her, but we're just friends, and I won't do anything to take it further."

"How does she feel about you? I mean, have the two of you talked about...you know, dating?"

"No. We've talked about everything else from processional wobble and the pyramids of Giza to our favorite television shows, but never about dating each other." She leaned back against the counter and crossed her arms. "What do you think? Do you think she likes me? You know, like that?"

"I know she likes you," Sandy said. "There may even be some hero worship going on there, too, but I'm not sure if she's interested in you." She gave a small smile. "It's not as if Nicole and I have ever sat down and had a heart-to-heart chat."

"You intimidate her. She thinks you don't like her."

"I don't know her well enough to like or dislike her. I just worry that you're going to be hurt by this." Sandy put her hand on her stomach. "Uh-oh."

Laurel was instantly alarmed. "What?"

"I got sick this morning."

Breathing a sigh of relief, Laurel relaxed. "Oh, the morning sickness has started?"

"Morning, afternoon, and just before I left to come here. I'd love to know if Mom went through it this bad, but I can't ask her now."

"Is it really bad?" Laurel asked, her earlier anger forgotten.

"Right now it's starting to act up again."

"Maybe you should pass on bowling tonight."

"No. I have soda crackers. They seem to help."

"All right, where are they?"

"In my jacket. I can get them."

There was a knock on the door, and Debbie Singer poked her head in. "What's going on? You two fighting?"

"No," the sisters answered in unison.

"Fine. Hurry up then, will ya?"

"We'll be out in a minute," Laurel said, waiting until Deb closed the door before addressing her sister. "How are you feeling?"

"Like I ate raw squid," Sandy said, rubbing her upset belly. "I don't know if this is normal."

"If you'd made an appointment with an obstetrician sooner, you'd know. Come on, I think you're sitting out tonight."

"Lots of pregnant women bowl. I'll be fine."

"All right, but promise me if it gets worse or you need to stop that you'll tell me."

"I will." Sandy reached for the door, then paused and looked at her sister. "Laurel, are we all right?"

"Of course. I just wish you'd be nicer to her." She put her arm around her sister's shoulders. "Come on, we have some loud-mouthed women who need to be taken down a peg or two."

Foster & Miller

# Chapter Eleven

Laurel sighed and threw the months-old magazine down. She hated waiting for anything, and doctor's offices were the worst for her. *What the hell is taking so long?* She reached for another magazine when the door opened and Sandy stepped out, still talking to the obstetrician. "Is everything all right?" she asked.

"Dr. Weiss, this is my sister, Laurel."

The doctor smiled and held out his hand. "Nice to meet you," he said. "You'll have to excuse me now. I've other patients to see. Miss Waxman, don't forget to make another appointment and make those changes I suggested."

"I will."

"So what'd he say?" Laurel asked as they headed to the reception desk to make her next appointment. "Is everything all right?"

"My iron is a little low, and I need to take multivitamins," Sandy said. "Other than that, I'm a perfectly healthy woman who's six weeks pregnant."

"Where to now?"

"The pharmacy, then I need to buy some new clothes."

"Excuse me?" Laurel put clothes shopping just below being stuck in a waiting room...but only just below. "You can't be getting bigger already."

"My boobs are," Sandy said. "They're sore, and Dr. Weiss said they're going to get even larger before I start to show."

"Bra shopping?"

"It won't take that long."

"You can't get in and out of a store in less than an hour, so who are you kidding?" Laurel asked. "Please tell me you're not dragging me to one of those lingerie boutiques."

"I was thinking of Moms To Be."

Laurel was wrong. There were things worse than waiting at a doctor's office, and for the next four hours, she experienced it firsthand. Sandy dragged her to the maternity store, the bookstore to buy a nutrition guide for pregnant women, and back to the maternity store to look around some more. By the time they were done, Laurel had seen all the maternity tops she ever wanted to see.

Nicole walked into the detective's bureau checking names on desk plates until she found the one she was looking for. "Detective Briggs?" The ruddy-faced man looked up from the paperwork he was reading. He looked her up and down, but Nicole ignored the leering smile that came to his face. "I'm Nicole Burke."

"Oh, yeah, the rookie from Hastings," he said, standing up and offering his beefy hand. "And a mighty pretty one, too." He winked at her. "Have a seat. What can I do for you?"

"I understand you're working on a missing persons case. Cheryl Wolf?"

His brow wrinkled. "I don't think...oh, yeah, elderly lady who took off for parts unknown." He pulled his keyboard out and called up the file. "Her friend reported her missing. Why are you asking?"

"The woman who reported her missing used to be my high school English teacher, and she's very worried about her friend," Nicole said. "Did you find out anything?"

He shook his head. "Just what I told her. I asked the woman who owns the place, and she told me Wolf just moved out. She showed me the room, and it looked like the woman was gone. The bed was made, the drawers and trash can were empty. No evidence of foul play." He leaned back in his chair. "You know how those snowbirds are. Got damn cold in December. I figure she headed for Arizona or Florida or wherever those old people go to get warm."

"And the landlady, Liza, she had no idea at all where Miss Wolf went?"

"Nope. Said the woman didn't tell her, just demanded her security back. She showed me an entry in her ledger and a carbon of the check." He sat up and put his forearms on his desk. "Miss Wolf moved out. Case closed."

"Did you pull the landlady's bank records to see if that check was ever cashed?"

"No."

"How can you close the case when you didn't even look at her account? That check is the only piece of physical evidence that supports the landlady's claim that Miss Wolf moved out."

"Don't tell me how to investigate my case, Rookie."

"Damn!" Nicole frantically wiped the spilled coffee off the printed recipe she had sitting on the counter. "Jim!"

"What'd you do? Set the kitchen on fire?" he asked as he entered the room.

"Ha, ha, very funny. Now don't just stand there. I need more paper towels."

Jim pulled a fresh roll from the pantry. "Can't we just order pizza again?"

"No. I didn't get up early and drive to a kosher butcher just to order pizza." She blotted the paper, thankful the ink had not smeared.

"Oh, that reminds me...Mark called while you were out. He asked me to go with him and his boys for a ski trip on Presidents Day weekend. Is it okay?"

Nicole tossed the wet paper towels in the trash. "You don't know how to ski."

"Mark's going to teach me."

Nicole smiled. "Sure. Sounds like lots of fun." She shook a wooden spoon at him. "Just be careful. I don't want you breaking a leg or anything." She turned back to the recipe. "Okay, let's see...put back chicken, add marjoram, garlic, and a small amount of parsley." She looked at the ingredient list again. "Jim, how much marjoram do I use?"

"Whatever it says. I don't know anything about Jewish cooking." He opened the refrigerator and pulled out a can of soda. "Why don't you call Sergeant Sexy and ask her?"

"Why don't you come over here and help me? And don't you dare call her that when she's here." She handed him the damp paper. "It just says marjoram. It doesn't say a pinch or a dash or anything. Do I put a little in or a lot?"

"Why didn't you pick something you knew how to cook?"

"Because I wanted to make sure it was kosher, and this looked easier than Greek-style lamb chops." She looked at the recipe again. "I knew I should have looked around at other Web sites. How can they tell you to add an ingredient and not tell you the amount? Well, let's hope it's not too much."

"If we fall on the floor holding our stomachs, you'll know it was too much," he said, ducking the backhand aimed at his midsection. "By the way, I need you to sign this."

"For what?"

"Just sign it, please?"

"You waited until I was a nervous wreck over dinner before springing this on me, didn't you?" She stirred the sauce, concerned that it wasn't thickening as the recipe said it would. "What is it?"

Jim pulled the folded paper from his back pocket. "It's a note from Principal Gordon."

"I'm going to kill you," she said, turning her attention away from the sauce. "Let me see."

"It wasn't my idea."

Nicole read the letter, her eyes growing wide. "You raided the girls' locker room?"

"I didn't raid it. I just stood watch while Doug and Jeremy went in. That's why I didn't get suspended."

"Two weeks of after-school detentions and probation for the rest of the school year. That's just great, Jim."

"Your sauce is boiling."

"Oh, damn." Nicole shut off the heat and moved the saucepan, quickly stirring the contents. "I'm really going to kill you." Fortunately, the sauce hadn't burned and had finally thickened to the point where she thought it was ready.

"I'm sorry. It's not like I did anything but watch the hall."

"At least it's not telling me you failed a drug test," she said, sighing and opening the junk drawer in search of a pen. "It was stupid."

"I can still go on the ski trip, right?"

"You shouldn't." Nicole turned her head when she heard the truck pull into the driveway. "She's here." She removed her apron and used her hands to smooth her hair and shirt. "Be on your best behavior. We'll talk about this…" She waved the paper at him "…later."

"I love you, Sis."

"Nice try. Set the table." Moving quickly, she reached the door and opened it just as Laurel was coming up the walk. "Hi."

"Hi." Heavy flakes of snow fell on her dark hair. "Think we're really in for it tonight."

Nicole looked around, surprised by how much snow had fallen since the last time she had checked. "We're gonna have a lot of accidents," she said, moving back to let her guest in.

"They're already telling people to stay off the streets if they don't have to be out," Laurel said, unzipping her jacket and brushing the snowflakes off her head.

Nicole took the jacket. "Do you want a towel?"

"Nah, that's the good thing about short hair. Dries quickly." Laurel sniffed the air. "Smells good."

"Chicken with picante sauce over rice," Nicole said. "I hope you like it."

"Don't blame me if you don't," Jim said as he put the plates on the table. "She's the cook tonight."

"I thought you said you didn't cook?"

"I don't," Nicole said. "But I figured you made me a nice meal. The least I could do was try to give you one." She felt warmth at the smile she received. "I can always order pizza or Chinese if I blew it."

"It smells wonderful," Laurel said. "And I love chicken picante."

Nicole smiled and gestured at the kitchen. "Have a seat, and I'll dish everything up."

"I'll serve," Jim said. "Laurel, would you like a drink?"

Laurel nodded. "Something hot if you have it."

"I'll get it for you," Nicole said.

"No, no, I'll get it," her brother said, moving to the coffee maker. "How do you take it?"

"Two sugars, no cream."

"I'll get one for you, too, Nickie."

Nicole walked over to where her brother was filling two mugs. "Laying it on a little thick, aren't you?" she asked quietly.

"Just showing you how sorry I am and how good I can be, now go sit."

"I still haven't decided on the ski trip." Nicole joined Laurel at the table and sat across from her. "I talked to Detective Briggs today."

"What'd he have to say?"

"He said he talked to the landlady, and she showed him where she wrote a refund check for Miss Wolf's security deposit." She took the mug Jim held out for her. "Thanks. I don't know, Laurel. I really believe Miss Schultz."

"Thanks, Jim," Laurel said when he handed her the mug. "I didn't bother trying to get any sleep after running around with Sandy, so I did a little checking for you. I talked to a friend of mine down at Social Services. She knows Liza Appleton."

"What'd she say?"

"She's referred people to that boarding house more than once. She thinks Appleton's a nice person."

"So no problems?"

Laurel shook her head. "No. Tanya said the boarding house may not be the best place in town to live, but it's clean and cheap, and Appleton provides furnishings and food, as well as transportation to things like doctor's appointments or the bank."

"Miss Schultz told me Liza was very friendly, and most people like her. Do you think this is just a waste of time?"

"I think you don't have enough information to tell."

Jim appeared with plates for each woman. "Nickie? If you don't mind, I'm going to eat dinner in the living room, so you two can talk cop talk."

"Sure," Nicole said, knowing her brother really just wanted to watch the show where the women run around in bikinis.

"Smells great," Laurel said as she picked up her fork.

"I hope you like it," Nicole said, privately worrying that she had used either too much or too little marjoram. She watched Laurel take her first bite and grinned when she gave her a thumbs-up.

"And you said you couldn't cook." Laurel scooped up another bite. "This is delicious."

"Thanks."

"I mean it. You can cook for me any time."

*I'd love to.* "I'm glad you liked it," Nicole said. "I was worried about it."

"I could tell. You watched me take just about every bite."

"I did?" It was only then that she realized she had stared at Laurel all through dinner, and worse yet, had been caught. Blushing furiously, she lowered her head and tried to cover her face with a napkin. "Sorry. I was worried because I wasn't sure how much marjoram to use."

"What's that?"

Nicole laughed. "If you don't know, then I guess it didn't matter. You want more coffee?"

Laurel put her hand over her mug. "I'm set."

"Then I guess I'd better get changed."

"Need help clearing the table?"

"Leave it for Jim," Nicole said as she stood up. "I'll explain later."


Nicole rang the doorbell again and buried her hands in her pockets to keep warm. Ten minutes of standing on the top step waiting for the door to be answered had left her chilled and wishing someone would hurry up and answer the door. "Come on, it's damn cold out here." Finally, the door opened, and an elderly man using a walker for support appeared. "Is Miss Schultz here?" she asked.

"I haven't seen her," the man said. "You'd have to ask Liza when she gets back."

"When was the last time you saw her?"

"Well, let's see. Liza talked to me at breakfast."

"No, I mean when did you last see Miss Schultz?"

"Oh, Martha. Let's see, yesterday? The day before?" He shook his head. "I'm sorry, young lady. I'm lucky I remember my name."

Nicole smiled at him and held out her hand. "I understand. I'm Nicole."

"Carl Greeley. If I see Martha, I'll tell her you stopped by."

"Okay, thanks, Mr. Greeley." Nicole headed back to her car but did not leave immediately. Instead, she pulled her notepad from the glove compartment and made a note about the date and time and with whom she had spoken. She started the engine to keep warm and carefully watched the front windows of the house for a few minutes to see if anyone peeked out. The house remained quiet, and Nicole left, returning at dusk to find an older car with fading red paint parked in the driveway. She scribbled down the license number and went to the door. This time when she pressed the doorbell, it was only a few seconds before a blond woman, who appeared to be in her late forties or early fifties, opened the door.

"Yes?"

"Hi. I'm looking for Martha. Is she around?"

"She's not here right now."

"Do you know when she'll be back?" Nicole asked, carefully watching the woman's face for any sign of deception.

"I'm not sure. Are you a relative?"

"No, just a friend. Will she be back tonight?"

"As I said, I don't know. If I see her, I'll let her know you were looking for her. Who should I say stopped by?"

"Nickie."

"Nickie…?"

"Just Nickie. She knows who I am," Nicole said, hesitant to give the woman her last name.

"Have a nice night."

"Yeah, thanks." Nicole walked back to her car, and this time, there was no doubt that she was being watched through a window to the right of the door. Something was definitely not right here. Miss Schultz had asked her to come back that day. Was expecting her. Feeling unsettled, she drove two blocks down the road and pulled over to make a notation in her notepad.

Nicole pulled into the bank parking lot and headed for the only car in the lot. She parked her cruiser so the driver's windows were next to each other and rolled her window down. A hand passed a steaming cup of coffee to her, and she accepted it gratefully. "Thanks."

"You're welcome," Laurel said. "I've got a cheese Danish over here, too, if you want some."

Nicole shook her head and took a sip of her coffee. "I went to the boarding house earlier, and Miss Schultz wasn't there." She frowned. "I don't like it. We'd made plans to meet. She was expecting me. I think Appleton did something to her."

"You can't prove it," Laurel said, turning the heater up another notch to compensate for the open window on a brisk February night. "Go back tomorrow and see if she's there."

"Would you go with me?" Nicole put her hands together and batted her eyes. "Please?"

Laurel almost agreed immediately but then she had another idea. "If I go with you there, will you go somewhere with me?"

"Sure, anywhere."

"Anywhere?"

"Um, maybe you should tell me where first."

"Don't you trust me?"

Nicole laughed. "I trust you with my life, but you have to tell me where first."

Laurel smiled and reached for her coffee. "Chicken. What's the matter? Worried I'll get you alone somewhere and jump on you?" She laughed, trying to pass her question off as a joke. "How about the Labrys, Wednesday night? It's not that busy on a weeknight, and we'll be able to get the pool table."

"I don't know," Nicole said. "I don't want to run into Rita."

"I'll make sure she doesn't bother you," Laurel said, surprised that her idea wasn't dismissed outright.

"They do have a good dance floor."

"Dance floor?" Laurel swallowed. "I don't dance."

"You can't dance?"

"You'd need your steel-toed boots if you danced with me."

Nicole grinned. "You got it. Steel-toed boots it is. Should we go in separate..." She stopped when the radio announced a robbery in progress at a nearby convenience store. Grabbing her mike, she responded and put the cruiser in gear while Laurel did the same.

"That's her," Nicole said, pointing to a woman picking a newspaper up off the porch of the house across the street.

"Okay, let's go get this over with."

Nicole looked at her friend. "You're not taking this serious, are you?"

"Sure I am."

Nicole shook her head and got out of the car without saying another word.

Laurel hurried after her and pulled her to a stop. "I know you're worried about your friend, but we can't lose sight of the fact that sometimes old people get confused. It happens. I don't want to make a judgment until I have more to go on."

"You didn't see Miss Schultz, Laurel. She was really scared. I tried to get her to leave that house, but she wouldn't. Told me she had to watch Liza. She was perfectly rational, and besides, she's not that old."

"I'm sorry if I sounded as if I'm not taking this seriously. You're a good cop, and I trust your instincts. If your gut feeling is that something's wrong, then we need to check it out."

They walked across the street and Nicole rang the bell. Liza Appleton answered the door and recognized Nicole immediately.

"Martha doesn't live here anymore," she said, not waiting for Nicole to say anything.

"When did she move?"

"Her friend Cheryl came and moved her out last night."

"Did she leave a forwarding address?

"Nope, just moved out." Liza abruptly stepped back inside and closed the door in their faces.

Laurel looked at Nicole and frowned. "Okay, now my gut's talking, too. Something is definitely not right here."

They turned and walked back to Nicole's car. "What's our next move?"

"We give this new info to Briggs and let him investigate. Officially, it's his case."

"He didn't do anything last time but play nice, nice with Liza Appleton. What makes you think he'll do any more this time?"

"We have to follow procedure, Nicole, it's his case. If he drops the ball, then we'll pick it up."

# Chapter Twelve

L aurel, I want you to take my car to the mechanic's Wednesday night, so he can work on it first thing Thursday morning," Elizabeth said. "I'm hearing a rattling sound."

"I can't," Laurel said. "I'm busy. Why can't Dad drop it off?"

"You know he can't drive at night anymore, and I need to run errands Wednesday afternoon."

"She means she needs to go play mahjong," Sandy said. "Ma, I'll take your car for you."

"Thank you, Sandy," Elizabeth said. "What's so important that you can't do it?" she asked, looking at her youngest daughter.

"I'm going out with a friend."

"That rookie?" Elizabeth asked. "Lucy Kramer said she saw you at the Golden Dragon with a woman."

"What makes you think it's Nicole? I do have other friends."

"If you're going out with the girl, then say it and bring her to dinner," Elizabeth said, shaking her head.

"Nicole and I aren't going out." She turned to her sister for help. "Sandy, tell her."

"They're just friends as far as I know," Sandy said. She walked over to the pantry and took out a sleeve of crackers.

"Don't spoil your dinner," Elizabeth said. "All I know is when your sister first met Theresa, that's all we heard about. Now every time I see her, it's Nicole this and Nicole that. If they're not going out, I'm sure it's not for lack of effort on my daughter's part."

Laurel decided it was time to change the subject. "Sandy's the one who broke the china cup you liked so much."

"Laurel forged your name on a note for school when she played hooky."

"If you two are going to start that, you can just get out of my kitchen." Elizabeth made a shooing motion with her hands. "Go, go. I swear, I can't carry on a conversation for ten minutes with you girls without the two of you starting on each other."

The sisters quickly made their escape into the den, paying no attention to the high-backed chair turned away from them. "Sorry about that," Laurel said. "I had to do something to get her off my back."

"She already knew about the china cup," Sandy said. "You know I was scared to death she'd put my being sick last week with eating crackers and figure it out."

"Why didn't you bring your own?"

"I did, but they're in my purse, and I needed some right then."

"I've been looking things up on the Internet," Laurel said. "Did you know there's a lollipop the doctor can prescribe that's supposed to help?"

"I'd rather not take any drugs," Sandy said. "How many times have they given women medications they said were safe only to find out later that they caused birth defects? I don't want to take the chance." She put her fist between her breasts. "First, I'm nauseated at least four times a day, and now I have heartburn that won't quit. What else do I have to look forward to?"

"How about explaining to your father what's going on?" Brian said as he swung around to face his daughters.

"Uh-oh," Laurel said, looking to her older sister for help. Unfortunately, Sandy had the same look on her face. "Um, Dad, we didn't know you were here."

"Obviously," he said. "So let's have it." When neither answered him immediately, he said, "All right, I see we have to do this the old-fashioned way. You, over there. You, sit there. Now, someone start talking."

Sandy saw no reason to deny what she knew he had heard. "I'm pregnant."

"When were you going to tell us?"

Sandy looked at Laurel for moral support. This was going to be so hard. "I didn't plan on telling you and Mom until I was further along because I'm giving the baby up for adoption." She looked at her father, her eyes pleading. "Please don't tell Ma yet. It'll just give her that many more months to stew and fret over losing her first grandchild."

Nicole sat at the bar sipping the screwdriver she had ordered. Every time the door opened, she would look up to see if it was Laurel, who was now almost half an hour late. Then she looked up and her jaw dropped. There was Laurel with her white shirt, thin leather tie, and black blazer standing in the doorway. *Oh, damn.* Nicole felt underdressed in her pale yellow button-down shirt and jeans. She took a healthy swallow of her drink to settle the swarm of butterflies that suddenly began fluttering in her stomach and waved Laurel over. "Hi."

"Hi. Sorry I'm late," Laurel said as she took the stool next to Nicole.

"That's okay. I was just watching the girls play pool."

Laurel looked over at the pool table. "Looks like we'll have to wait to play." She nodded at Nicole's drink. "What's that?"

Nicole held up her half-empty glass. "Screwdriver."

"That's one way to get your vitamin C," Laurel said, motioning for the bartender. "Bottle of Miller if you have it."

"Three fifty," the bartender said as she pulled a bottle from the cooler and opened it. "Glass?"

"No, thanks." Laurel put a five-dollar bill on the counter and took her beer. "I thought it would be quieter here tonight."

Nicole looked around. "It's not too busy. Plenty of empty tables."

Laurel pointed at one near the pool table. "Want to go over there?"

"Sure." Nicole picked up her drink and followed Laurel to the table, smiling as she noticed the heads turning to get a better look at her companion. *Eat your hearts out, ladies. She's with me.* "You want me to put quarters up for a game?"

Laurel looked at the table. "There's already quite a few waiting to play. Why don't we wait and see if it dies down?"

Nicole pulled out the chair and sat down. "It could be a while."

"That's all right," Laurel said, taking the seat opposite her. "We could always play darts or pinball if you're bored."

"Me? No, I'm fine," Nicole said. "You sure you don't dance?"

Laurel smiled and took a long pull on her beer. "Not a step, but I'm sure there's at least a dozen women here who would be more than happy to dance with you."

Nicole shook her head. "It's not me they're looking at."

"Oh, please. If I got up and went to the bathroom, there'd be at least two women over here flirting with you before I got back." She nodded at a young woman standing near the jukebox. "She's been watching you."

"Not my type," Nicole said.

"You know you still haven't told me what your type is."

Nicole finished her drink. "Uh-huh, and you haven't told me yours." She turned her head to look at the woman by the jukebox. "Too skinny."

"All right." Laurel looked around. "What about that one?"

"Too butch."

Laurel took a sip of her beer as her eyes swept the room. "That one?"

"Nah. Too femme."

"You're just not going to tell me, are you?"

Nicole stood up and reached for her empty glass. "It's more fun to make you guess," she said. "I'll get this round." She went to the bar, returning with fresh drinks and a pocket of quarters. She stopped at the pool table and placed two quarters with a penny on top at the end of the line of quarters. "Six people ahead of us," she said as she set the drinks down. "I put a penny on ours, so we can tell when it's our turn."

"Good idea," Laurel said. "Interested in a game of pinball?"

"Sure."

They played several games of pinball before it was their turn at the table. Nicole wasn't very good at pool, so she was happy when the person running the table suggested they play partners. It was a good game, though they lost easily to the other women. They returned to their table to find their drinks gone. "Knew we should have taken them with us," she said.

"I think it's my turn to buy the round," Laurel said. "Do we need more quarters?"

Nicole shook her head. "I'm all pinballed out, and we'll never beat those two at pool."

"All right, I'll be right back."

While Laurel was off getting their drinks, Nicole watched the couples on the dance floor. She wanted to dance, but there was only one person in the bar whom she wished to be with, and Laurel had told her unequivocally that dancing wasn't an option. Turning her head toward the bar, she watched as a blonde with clothes far too tight sidled up next to Laurel and began talking to her. Jealousy burned through Nicole, and she took an instant dislike for the woman talking to Laurel. When the woman's hand began sliding up and down Laurel's arm, Nicole stood with the intention of going over but stopped. *This is crazy. She's not my girlfriend, and if she wants to flirt with someone, it's none of my business.* Now angry with herself, Nicole sat back down and turned her chair, so she couldn't see the pair at the bar.

"What's wrong?" Laurel asked as she set the drinks down and took her seat. "You look like you're about to put your fist through a wall."

Nicole picked up her drink and took several healthy swallows before answering. "Nah, just thinking about how much of a meat rack this place is."

"Yeah, I know what you mean. Can't even go get a drink without someone hitting on you. Did you see that twit who came up when I was waiting for our drinks?" Laurel shook her head and smiled. "I mean, she heard me order two drinks, and she still asked me out. How stupid is that?"

"What'd you say?" Nicole asked, not sure if she wanted to hear the answer.

"I told her I thought it was pretty tasteless to ask me out when I was already with someone and that you had a jealous streak a mile long."

Nicole reached for her drink again. "You could have said yes if you wanted to."

Laurel shook her head. "She's not my type."

"You ever going to tell me what your type is?" Nicole asked, feeling her anger ebb.

"As soon as you tell me yours," Laurel countered. "I'm not into blondes with egos the size of the Superdome."

Surprised by how much of her drink was already gone, Nicole pushed her glass away and looked down at the table. "You sure I can't talk you into one dance?"

"I have no rhythm and two left feet. I'd probably step all over your toes."

Feeling a courage aided by the alcohol, Nicole raised her head and looked into soft brown eyes. "I'd be willing to take the chance."

Laurel looked at the dance floor, then back to her. "One dance and you promise not to laugh at me."

Nicole hopped from her chair and held out her hand. "I promise," she said, feeling the warmth of Laurel's fingers within hers as she led them to the dance floor. They found a spot in the back corner, the multi-colored disco lights bouncing off them and the wall as the beat vibrated through the floor.

"I'm really no good at this," Laurel said, standing completely still.

Nicole began moving to the upbeat music. "Relax," she said. "No one's watching us. Just do what I do." She smiled and held her arms out, taking Laurel's hands in her own. "That's it. Just feel the music, and let your body move."

"I feel stupid."

"You're doing fine," Nicole said, silently agreeing that her friend had absolutely no sense of rhythm. The song ended and was replaced by a popular love song that pulled couples to the dance floor. When Laurel tried to pull away, Nicole tightened her hold and moved closer. "Relax," she said, sliding her arms around the firm waist and resting her head on Laurel's shoulder. She felt hands go around her neck and closed her eyes, enjoying the warmth beneath her cheek and inhaling the scent of Laurel's perfume. "That's it," she whispered, gently swaying to the music.

"You're a good dancer," Laurel said, her smoky voice caressing Nicole's ear.

"It's the company," Nicole said, splaying her fingers out and gently pressing against Laurel's back. "Thank you."

"For what?"

"This. I know you didn't want to dance."

"How can I resist those baby blues?" Laurel asked.

Nicole felt fingers slide into her short hair, and it took all of her willpower not to kiss the neck only inches from her lips. *I wish we could just stay like this*. The lyrics and music were lost to her; all that mattered was the feeling of Laurel in her arms, the strong heartbeat beneath her ear, the fingers that continued to play with the back of her hair, the feel of soft breath against her cheek. The song ended far too quickly, and it was with great reluctance that she pulled back.

"Last call, ladies," the DJ announced as the lights in the bar came up, and the dance lights were shut off.

"I suppose we should get going," Laurel said, stepping back and putting her hands in her pockets.

"Did you want to finish your drink?" Nicole asked, silently disappointed at the loss of contact.

Laurel shook her head. "I'm all set. You?"

"I think I've had enough," she said. "Hungry? We can go to one of the all-night diners and grab a bite to eat."

"Anything you want," Laurel said. "We can always go back to my place and play a few games of chess if you're up to it."

Not wanting the evening to end, Nicole readily agreed.

"I am in so much trouble," Nicole said when she entered her bedroom, winking a hello to her cat lying on the bed. "What am I going to do, Puddy?" Kicking off her sneakers, she stripped and crawled into bed. "I almost kissed her tonight," she said, absently petting the cat's head. "I work with her. I can't be attracted to her." Sighing, she reached over and shut off the lamp. "I almost beat her tonight. Got her in check twice before she put me in checkmate. One of these days, I'm gonna beat her." Her only answer was Puddy's contented purring. "I'm falling for her." She exhaled slowly and looked up at the darkened ceiling. "God, how could I not? Everything about her just makes me want to...ah, damn. I never should have gone to the Labrys with her tonight. I never should have danced with her." She rolled over and punched her pillow. "That's me, Puddy. Always wanting what I can't have."

"Can't you do anything?" Nicole asked, annoyed by the detective's apparent lack of interest. "I know something happened to her."

"I talked to Miss Appleton," Detective Briggs said, leaning back in his chair. "She said Miss Wolf came and picked up your friend, and she hasn't seen them since." He picked up an autographed baseball from its holder on his desk. "There's no crime here, Rookie. Sounds like two old ladies didn't like where they were living and moved."

"After everything I told you, you still believe her?"

He took the printed report and held it out for her. "As far as I'm concerned, the case is closed. You want to keep investigating it, be my guest."

Nicole snatched the report out of his hand and stormed away without saying a word. The man was an idiot if he couldn't see that more investigating was necessary to find out what was going on in that house. She jerked the door open and headed for her car. "Pig-headed fool."

She knew she was too angry to go home and sleep and opted to drive to the stable and see if she could catch Laurel before she went home. The drive to the stable didn't take long, and she was relieved to see Laurel's truck parked behind her tack shed.

Cheyenne nickered when she saw Nicole and stuck her head over the fence in an attempt to coax a few extra carrots out of her. "Okay, okay, but just a few," Nicole said and grabbed a handful of the treats from the burlap sack that was just inside the shed door.

Feeding the big mare had a calming effect on Nicole, but she was not quite over her anger by the time Laurel returned with an empty wheelbarrow. It was clear Laurel could tell she was upset because her brow furrowed when she saw her.

"Something bothering you?"

Nicole nodded. "I can't get Miss Schultz off my mind. I talked to Briggs again this morning, but he's written her off and closed the case. Told me that the Appleton woman said Miss Wolf came back and moved her out."

"We told him that."

"I know. He's not going to do a damn thing. Handed the file to me and said if I wanted to keep investigating, I was on my own."

"*We're* on our own," Laurel said. "I'm in this with you, remember?"

Nicole slammed her locker, unaware that Laurel had just entered the locker room. "Damn it!"

"What's wrong?"

"Frustration." Nicole sighed. "The Appleton woman won't let me in to talk to any of her boarders, and there's not a damn thing I can do about it."

Laurel patted her shoulder. "I've got some news that might make you feel better." She grinned and held up a manila folder. "I got 'em."

"The bank records?"

"Yep, and the refund check that Appleton supposedly gave to Miss Wolf was never cashed."

"I knew it! And if Briggs had just done his job, Miss Schultz might still be here."

"This doesn't prove anything yet because people sometimes hold checks a while before cashing them. But they're starting an investigation on Appleton, and this time, they're taking it seriously."

Nicole carefully looked over the chessboard, her excitement growing with each passing second. "Check."

"I think I'm in trouble here," Laurel said as she moved her king out of danger.

Smiling broadly, Nicole moved her queen. "Check."

"Definitely in trouble." She moved her bishop to block the threat of Nicole's queen.

"Oh, no, you don't." Nicole used her rook to take out the last black bishop. "Check."

"You're getting too good at this," Laurel said, moving her king one space to the right.

"I did it," Nicole said, moving her knight. "Checkmate!"

Smiling and nodding, Laurel tipped her king onto its side. "Good game."

Excited, Nicole jumped up from her seat. "I really did it! I beat you. I won."

Laurel rose, as well. "Yes, you did. You won fair and square."

Without thinking, Nicole wrapped her arms around Laurel and hugged her. "I can't believe I won."

Just as Nicole acted without thought, the moment broke through Laurel's defenses, and she did what her heart had been begging her to do for so long. Cupping Nicole's face, she brushed their lips together, then returned for a kiss, closing her eyes when she felt Nicole respond. She didn't know whose lips parted first, but when their tongues touched, she moaned and pulled Nicole closer. She felt hands pushing her away and pulled back, feeling slightly dazed from the kiss. The euphoria quickly ended, however, when she saw the sad look in Nicole's eyes.

"Damn it," Nicole said softly, lowering her head and stepping back. "I'm sorry. That wasn't supposed to happen."

"Why?" Laurel's heart began to pound as a feeling of dread overcame her. Sad blue eyes looked back at her.

"We can't," Nicole said. "I'm so sorry." She turned away and leaned her hands on the counter, lowering her head. "I should go."

"Wait. Let's talk about this." Laurel stepped forward and put her hand on Nicole's shoulder. "Nicole, please."

"Damn it." Nicole walked into the living room, sat down in the recliner, and put her elbows on her knees, her eyes never leaving the carpet.

Laurel sat on the couch opposite her, desperately trying to keep her emotions in check. "Why?"

"We work together," Nicole said, not looking up.

"So?"

"So I can't take that chance." Burying her face in her hands, Nicole took several shuddering breaths before continuing. "I need this job, Laurel. If I got involved with you, then we broke up, I'd never be able to stay with the force. I know that. It happened before with Rita."

"If I did anything…"

"It's not you. It's me. I know myself. I'd never be able to face going to work day after day and having you there."

"So, because you're afraid it wouldn't work out, you're not willing to even take the chance?"

"I can't. You're my best friend, and I treasure that friendship. If we crossed that line and it didn't work, I'd lose that, too. I couldn't go back to just being friends." She wiped at her eyes. "I'm sorry. The last thing I want to do is hurt you."

"If it didn't work, I'll switch to another shift. Our working together doesn't have to be an obstacle."

"But it is. Don't you see? I wouldn't ask you to do that, and even if you did, your sister is a lieutenant and your uncle is chief. It'd be too hard for me. I'd have to quit, and I can't afford to lose this job. It's not just about me. I have responsibilities. I have to raise my brother and put him through school." She shook her head. "I'm not stupid. I knew you were attracted to me, and I should have backed off then, but I…I just couldn't. I care for you. I like hanging out with you and being friends, but I just can't let it go any further."

Trying to ignore the pain in her heart, Laurel said, "I understand."

"Do you?"

"Our friendship is important to me, too. I don't want to lose it, either."

"I'm sorry, Laurel."

"So am I."

"I...I should go."

Laurel stood up and followed her to the door. "Nicole?" She waited until the other woman turned to face her. "We're still friends?" She received a nod. "Good."

"I'm sorry."

"Hey, in a few weeks we'll probably be laughing over this," Laurel said, though she did not believe that for a second. "I'll see you at the alley tomorrow?"

Nicole gave a shaky nod. "Sure."


"Who the hell is it?" Sandy asked as she pulled her robe closed and walked toward her front door while wiping the sleep from her eyes.

"Laurel."

"It's almost two in the morning," Sandy said as she unlocked the front door and opened it. "What's—" She stopped when she saw the shattered look on her younger sister's face. "Sis? What's wrong?"

"I...I didn't know where else to go," Laurel said as she stepped inside, her eyes red and puffy.

"What happened?"

Laurel wiped at her eyes. "I kissed her."

"Come here," Sandy said, pulling Laurel into her arms and leading her to the couch. "Tell me what happened."

"She...she doesn't want me," Laurel said, curling into a ball and leaning against her. "She wants to be...friends."

"Oh," Sandy whispered as her sister began crying in earnest. "Oh, Sis." She held Laurel as the tears continued to fall. "It's all right, let it out. I've got you."

"It hurts so much," Laurel cried, holding onto Sandy's robe with her fist. "She's the one, Sandy. She's the one, and she...she doesn't want me."

"Did she say why?"

"Because we work together. I love her, Sandy. I love her so much."

Sandy tightened her hold and began rocking. "I know you do. I know." She stroked her sister's short black hair. "Shh, it's going to be all right. You'll work through this." She felt Laurel shake her head. "Yes, you will. I know it hurts now, but it'll get better, I promise."

# Chapter Thirteen

N icole gripped the steering wheel, looking up at the neon sign over the bowling alley. *I should go in. They're expecting me.* It was the same thought she had ten minutes before, yet worry over facing Laurel kept her pinned in the car. She continued to fret about the situation until she was jolted by a tapping on the car window.

"Are you ready to kick the Public Works's ass tonight?" Debbie Singer asked.

Putting on her best smile, Nicole nodded and opened the door. "Hi, Deb. I was um…just psyching myself up."

"Glad to hear it. My thumb's a little sore, so I'm not sure how much good I'll be tonight."

Nicole opened the back door and retrieved her bowling bag. "Sorry to hear that."

"That's the problem with a desk job," Debbie said. "Paper cuts. So, how are things with you and Laurel?"

*Oh, no, please don't grill me tonight.* "Things are fine. She's a good friend."

"That's not quite what I meant."

"Oh?" Nicole began walking toward the glass doors, hoping the sooner she got inside, the sooner Sergeant Singer would find something else to do other than try to play matchmaker.

"Come on, Nicole. You can't tell me you two don't have something going on."

"She's my superior. You know the department's policy on that." *Please change the subject.*

"Policy and reality are two different things."

"My, it really is cold tonight." Reaching the doors, Nicole opened one and held it for Debbie to enter.

"I have to say I haven't seen Laurel this happy in a long time."

Nicole cringed. Obviously, she hadn't seen her since the night before. "Deb, nothing's going on between us."

"Really?" Debbie leaned in close. "Are you interested?"

*More than I can believe.* After getting home the previous night, Nicole cried on Puddy's fur until daylight and suffered another crying jag in the afternoon. "I don't date cops, Deb."

"Your loss. Oh, here we are. Lanes one and two." Debbie waved at the woman milling about. "Hi, Laurel."

"Hey, Deb." Laurel's eyes met Nicole's. "Hi."

"Hi." *She looks tired.* Feeling guilty, Nicole looked down at the worn carpet. *I should have been up front with her from the beginning. Now I'll be lucky if she stays my friend.* "Um, excuse me." Setting her bag down, she took off to the bathroom, aware before she reached the door that Laurel was following her. She went inside, unsure if she was pleased or disappointed that they were the only two in the room.

"Nicole."

"I'm sorry." Her eyes remained focused on the tile floor.

Gentle fingers tugged on Nicole's chin. "Hey. Look at me." Lifting her head, Nicole found herself looking into sad eyes. "Either you're practicing to be a raccoon for Halloween or you had just as hard a night as I did."

"I didn't mean to hurt you."

Laurel gave a small smile, her fingers remaining on Nicole's chin. "I know that. I kissed you, remember? I'm the one who should be apologizing."

Feeling disconcerted by the closeness, Nicole stepped back, breaking their contact. "I should have told you how I felt." Again she looked at the floor. "And you didn't do anything that I didn't want."

"So, no matter how we feel, nothing can happen because we work together?"

"I can't." Nicole took a shaky breath. "I ruined our friendship, didn't I?" She found herself wrapped up in strong arms. "I don't want to lose you."

"Shh, you won't," Laurel said. "I promise."

They separated quickly at the sound of the door opening but not before Sandy saw the embrace. "I'd better get ready," Nicole said.

"You don't—" Laurel began, but Nicole had already moved past her and through the door. "What?"

"I never figured you for a masochist," Sandy said, crossing her arms and leaning against the wall. "What the hell was that?"

"We were talking."

"Looked more like hugging to me."

Laurel scowled and crossed her arms in an unconscious imitation of her older sister. "Did you come in here for a reason?"

"Other than I figured you two had been in here long enough?"

"I don't need a babysitter, Sandy."

"You don't need someone who just plays with your feelings, either."

"Nicole's not responsible for my feelings. She has her reasons, no matter how stupid I think they are."

Sandy's stance softened. "Aw, Sis, back away from this now before you're hurt more than you already are. She's not worth it."

"How do you know?" Laurel snapped. "You don't know anything about her."

"I know you cried last night because of her. I know you took a chance and told her how you felt and she repaid you by stomping all over your heart. I know—"

"Enough." Laurel turned her back to her sister. "She didn't stomp all over my heart, as you so delicately put it. She honestly tried to explain her feelings to me. It's not her fault it wasn't what I wanted to hear." Anger was easier to deal with than pain, and Laurel latched onto it. "I turned to you last night for comfort, not so you could throw it back in my face."

"I'm not trying to throw it back in your face. I'm trying to make you see what all this is doing to you."

Laurel took a shaky breath, refusing to meet her sister's concerned gaze. "I just have to learn to keep my feelings to myself," she said. "She's my friend, and I'm not going to lose that."

The muffled sound of the announcer calling practice time on the lanes filtered through the closed bathroom door. Sandy moved forward and put her hand on Laurel's shoulder. "I hate to see you hurting."

Wiping at the tear that escaped from her eye, Laurel nodded. "I know, Sis. It'll get better."

Elizabeth Waxman had enough. "Laurel Beth."

"What?"

"I didn't spend all that time making dinner, so you could push it around your plate."

Sighing, Laurel dropped her fork. "I'm just not hungry."

"Sweetheart, what's wrong?" Brian asked. He was concerned by his younger daughter's moodiness.

"Nothing, Dad."

"Did you and Nicole have a fight?" Elizabeth asked. "You haven't mentioned her at all today, and usually, her name is every other word out of your mouth."

"We didn't have a fight."

"So why the long face?" Brian asked.

"Nothing's wrong," Laurel said, her chair scraping against the hardwood floor as she stood up. "Nicole's a friend, nothing more." She swallowed against the lump in her throat. "Just a friend, got it?"

"Your mother and I are just worried about you."

"There's nothing to worry about." Laurel looked at her sister. "Sandy, tell them there's nothing to worry about."

"There's nothing to worry about," Sandy said in an unconvincing tone.

"You're a lot of help. Mom, Dad, really, everything's fine." Reaching down, Laurel picked up her plate. "I'm not hungry, and I'm probably a bit tired. That's all."

Nicole moped around the house, the home she had grown up in, feeling very empty with Jim off on his ski trip. Gomer and Puddy had provided some distraction but not enough to shake the pain in her heart. Several times, she had picked up the phone to call Laurel only to stop herself before she could dial the familiar number. She missed their chats but believed space was what was needed between them now. The friendship could return with time, she assured herself. Right now they both had to learn to accept what would never be. Needing companionship, she walked over to the window and picked up the multi-colored cat from the fleece perch. "Come here, sweetie." She smiled at the loud purr she received as she settled into the recliner. "You think Jim's having a good time on his ski trip? I bet he is. I could have been at Laurel's right now, playing chess or cards or just talking." She moved a paw intent on kneading her breast. "This really sucks, you know?"

The phone rang and her heart began to pound. *What if it's her?* She picked up the phone and glanced at the caller ID readout. It wasn't Laurel. The call was from a payphone.

"Hello?"

"Nickie Burke?"

"This is she."

"I'm Sheila Hadley, Martha's friend."

Nicole sat up straight, her breath catching. "Have you heard from her?"

"No, but she left a letter for you with me. She said if anything happened to her, I was to get it to you, and I was to make sure I didn't put it in the outgoing mail for Liza to see. I'm sorry I haven't called sooner, but Liza's been sticking close to the house, and I haven't been able to slip out to get to a phone."

"Do you have the letter with you?"

"Yes."

Nicole jumped from her chair and ran to grab her coat from the closet. This letter just might be the break she'd been waiting for.

"Where are you?"

"I'm at the payphone in front of the Wash N Dry on Lincoln. Do you know the place?"

"I sure do. Wait inside, and I'll be there in about fifteen minutes."

She shrugged into her coat and was out the door in a flash.

Nicole entered the Wash N Dry and saw a lone woman sitting on the far side of the room. "Mrs. Hadley?" The woman nodded and Nicole sat down next to her. "You said on the phone that you have a letter for me."

"I didn't believe her, and now she's gone, too." Sheila blinked back a tear. "Now, I don't know what to think." She reached into her purse and pulled out an envelope addressed to Nickie Burke. "I'm scared. I've lived there for almost five years, and I never gave it a second thought when someone moved away. Now, I realize that the ones who just suddenly left were the ones who had no family to check on them. Me, I have children and grandchildren. I guess that kept me safe. But if she ever suspects that I know what's going on...."

Don't worry, Mrs. Hadley. I'm getting you out of there today. I just wish I'd gotten Miss Schultz out when she told me what she suspected." Nicole accepted the letter, opened it, and began to read:

```
Dear Nickie,
     I'm going to find out what happened to Cheryl or die
trying. No one believes me, and Liza is getting more
agitated with each passing day because I won't stop
pursuing this. Today was really bad, and I actually
thought she was going to hit me.
     Please, Nickie, if something happens to me, stop her
from doing it to anyone else. I'm scared, but I'm not
going to run. Someone has to do something, and I guess
it's me. Cheryl was all I had, and with her gone, nothing
seems to matter anymore. I have to make Liza pay for what
she did to her. I can't live with myself if I don't.
     If I'm suddenly gone and Liza tells you that I moved
out, don't believe her. I swear to you that I will not
leave here without telling you first. If I disappear,
then it is because she killed me, too. I hope I'm wrong,
but I don't think so.
     I'm counting on you to put her away. That's why I
wanted to write this letter. I want to make sure you
would have proof that something deadly is going on here.
     God Speed,
     Martha
```

There was no doubt in Nicole's mind now that Miss Schultz had been a victim of foul play. She put the letter back in the envelope and stuck it in her jacket pocket. "Do you need a place to stay?"

Mrs. Hadley shook her head. "I called my daughter and told her I'm coming for a visit." She patted her purse. "Already bought my train ticket."

"Good. Let's get you home to pack a bag, and I'll give you a lift to the station."

Laurel read Martha Schultz's letter again and frowned. "I just hope this is enough to nail that bitch." She handed the letter back to Nicole. "I'm assuming you already turned in the original."

Nicole nodded. "I gave it to Lieutenant Babbet in homicide. He said it was enough to get a search warrant. Said they would request the cadaver dog from Ripley because it's unlikely she'd have been able to take the bodies away from the house without being seen. He thinks they may be buried in her back yard. Do you suppose they'll let us go with them when they search the place?"

"I don't see why we wouldn't be allowed to observe as long as we don't get in their way. If it wasn't for you, there wouldn't be a case."

Nicole shoved the letter in her pocket and took a sip of her coffee. "Why didn't I insist she come with me that day we talked? This didn't have to happen."

Laurel placed her hand on Nicole's shoulder. "Don't beat yourself up over this."

"I can't help it. She'd be alive today if it wasn't for me."

"No!" Laurel tightened her grip on Nicole's shoulder. "Martha was a grown woman, and she chose to stay in that house. Let's put the blame where it really belongs. Liza Appleton."

Nicole looked around the large backyard and saw how it would be possible to bury bodies without being seen. The yard was enclosed with a six-foot fence, and the fence was lined with evergreen trees, effectively hiding the yard from prying eyes. Later in the day, the handler would be here with the dog, and she suspected it would find several bodies buried in the secluded yard. Too many old people had disappeared from this house without a trace for it to be a coincidence.

The forensic team finished with the house and was now about to cut the lock off the garden shed. No bodies had been found so far, but they had confiscated several boxes from the basement that contained personal items from some of the missing tenants. Appleton claimed that the items were in storage until the owners came back for them. Nicole stuck her hands in her pocket, a shiver running through her body.

"You cold?" Laurel asked when she saw the visible shudder.

"Yeah, but it's more than that." Nicole's eyes never left the garden shed. "My gut tells me she's in there."

They heard officers speaking rapidly in the shed, then Lieutenant Babbet emerged and motioned them over. "We've found the body of an elderly woman in there, Burke. I need you to take a look and verify if it's your missing friend." He handed her some covers to slip over her shoes. "Don't touch anything, just look."

Nicole's stomach twisted in knots as she put on the booties. She wanted to scream out that she didn't want to see Miss Schultz like that, but she couldn't. She was a cop surrounded by other cops. She would be professional and hold herself together if it killed her.

The shed was dark inside, the only light coming from the open door and the flashlights the two men inside were holding. There was an open trunk against the back wall, and Nicole's feet felt like lead as she walked toward it. When she was close enough, she forced herself to look down. Miss Schultz was lying on her side, her legs folded up against her. Her body was slightly twisted, and her face was clearly visible. Nicole was grateful that Miss Schultz did not appear to have been brutalized. "That's her. Martha Schultz."

"Thank you, Officer Burke. That's all I need from you right now. You can go."

Nicole didn't have to be told twice. She turned in place and hurried from the small enclosure. As soon as she saw Laurel's supportive face, she almost burst out crying, but she managed to hold it in.

"Was it her?"

Nicole nodded and kept walking, wanting to get as far away from the grisly scene as possible.

Laurel fell in step and they walked silently from the yard. "Are you all right?" she finally asked as they approached Nicole's car.

"I'll be fine. It was just a shock to see her like that."

"What say you come to the stables with me? It might help take your mind off unpleasant things, and besides, Cheyenne misses you."

"I miss her, too, and you're probably right, I do need a distraction right about now. Okay."

Laurel smiled and opened Nicole's car door for her. "Great. I have to stop for gas, so I'll see you there."

Nicole nodded and climbed into her car. She waited until Laurel pulled away before she started her car. Tears flowed down her cheeks, and she leaned over the steering wheel and gave in to them. She didn't understand why this was hitting her so hard. Martha Schultz had been her teacher, and she liked her, but they were never close. Not even friends. She reached into her glove compartment and pulled out a tissue. She wished she had been able to give in to the need to let Laurel comfort her, but she couldn't do it. It wasn't fair to either of them. She slammed her fist down on the steering wheel. "Damn it! Why do I have to need her so much?" She blew her nose and dabbed at her eyes and tried to pull herself together. No longer sure whether it was such a good idea to agree to meet Laurel at the stable, she pulled away from the curb, unsure of where she was going, but needing to do something.

Laurel scooped up the last of the soiled straw from Cheyenne's stall and deposited it in the wheelbarrow. The big mare nudged her back, almost pushing her over. She turned around and put her hands on her hips. "You're not getting any treats until your pal Nicole gets here. She loves to pamper you, so you're just going to have to be patient."

Cheyenne nudged her again and she laughed. "Okay, okay, if she's not here by the time I get back from the compost heap, I'll give you a little something to tide you over." Laurel glanced at her watch, her brow furrowing. "Where are you?" Something wasn't right, and she gripped the handles of the wheelbarrow, determined to complete her chores as quickly as possible so she could find Nicole.

Laurel breathed a sigh of relief as she rounded the corner of the arena and saw Nicole's car parked next to the tack shed. She left the wheelbarrow by the shed and joined Nicole at the stall. "I was beginning to think you'd changed your mind."

"I needed some time to get my head together."

Laurel pointed to the burlap sack of carrots. "Well, since you're here now, make yourself useful. Cheyenne's been waiting an hour and a half for you to spoil her." She leaned against the doorway and smiled as she watched Nicole feed Cheyenne handfuls of carrots. "I know that was hard on you back there. If you need to talk, I'm here."

"I'm okay, really."

"Okay, but if you change your mind, the offer stands." Laurel entered the stall and pulled a hoof pick out of her back pocket and proceeded to clean Cheyenne's hoofs. It was nice having Nicole here again. Perhaps things were finally going to start getting back to normal between them. "How would you like to ride with me for a bit?" She nodded toward the next stall over. "I'm taking care of Rabbit's Foot over there for the next couple of weeks, and he could use a bit of exercise."

Nicole's eyes tracked to the dapple gray gelding. "What is he, a Clydesdale?"

Laurel laughed. "He's not that big."

"He's huge. What is he?"

"Thoroughbred/Percheron mix. Bob takes him to three-day events. He's a great jumper."

"I'll go, but only if I get to ride Cheyenne."

Laurel grinned. "Chicken."

"Yep, and not too proud to admit it."

Laurel dug a key out of her pocket and opened the tack shed in front of the next stall. It only took a few minutes, and she had the two horses ready to go. She led the way to a well-worn trail that worked its way around the stable and continued alongside a small creek that was partly iced over in the shallow areas. It was a pretty setting, and they rode for several minutes in silence until the trail widened enough to where they could ride side by side.

Nicole watched a squirrel dash across their path and disappear in the snow-covered foliage. "I bet it's really pretty here in the spring."

Laurel nodded. "It is." A snowflake landed on her cheek and Laurel looked up at the sky and frowned. "It wasn't supposed to snow until tonight. We'd better turn back before we get caught out here in a storm."

They started back toward the stable, and by the time they arrived, the occasional flake had turned into a steady dusting.

"Looks as if we got back just in time," Laurel said as she pulled the saddle off the gray gelding and began to brush him down.

Nicole followed suit, and soon the horses were back in their respective stalls munching on a new supply of tasty carrots.

Laurel stowed the tack away and brushed the snowflakes out of her hair. "Why don't you come to my place after we finish here, and I'll fix us something to eat?"

"I don't think that's such a good idea."

The words stung, and Laurel felt hurt and anger well up inside. "Why not? You think if I get you alone at my place I'll try something?"

"Of course not. I just think it would be hard...for both of us."

"I thought we were going to stay friends, Nicole. Friends talk and hang out together."

"What do you call what we were just doing?"

"Fine. Let's keep hanging out then."

Nicole sighed. "Laurel..."

"What? Why does it matter if we're hanging out here or hanging out there?"

"I'm sorry if this hurts, but it's what I need to do. Maybe I don't trust myself, okay?"

Laurel turned and grabbed the wheelbarrow. "Maybe you're just making excuses."

"Maybe I'm just trying to keep us from making a mistake that would completely ruin our friendship."

"A mistake." Laurel put the wheelbarrow into the tack shed. "Why are you so sure it would be a mistake?" She snapped the lock shut. "Fine. Whatever. Do what you need to do. I'll see you at work."

Whatever else Nicole had to say was ignored as Laurel stormed to her truck. When she reached the old Ford, she slammed her door. "Fuck!"

*Foster & Miller*

# Chapter Fourteen

I'm not playing with you anymore, you cheat," Laurel said as she slammed the cards down on the table.

"I don't have to cheat," Sandy said. "You're a lousy cribbage player."

"Am not."

"Are too."

Laurel folded her arms over her chest and stuck out her lower lip.

Sandy couldn't help but laugh. "You look like such a baby when you pout."

"I'm not pouting."

"Yes, you are."

"Am not."

"I wish you would just get over her and stop being such a grump all the time."

"I'm not a grump."

"Yes, you are."

"Am not."

Sandy threw up her arms in defeat. "Okay, you're little Mary Sunshine. Now can we finish the game?"

Laurel slumped down in her chair. "Have I really been that bad?"

"Afraid so, Little Sis."

"I miss her."

"It's not like you don't see her every day at work."

Laurel shook her head. "It's not the same. We used to talk, you know? I mean really talk. Now we acknowledge each other. We're pleasant. But we don't talk."

"Maybe it's for the best. You need to get on with your life."

"But I want Nicole to be a part of my life." She gathered up the cards and began to shuffle them. "She's made it clear we can't be lovers, but I don't understand why we can't be friends."

"She said you can't be friends?"

"She says she wants to stay friends, but every time I ask her to do something with me, she says no. It's been two months since she's come to the stable to see Cheyenne." Laurel looked up at Sandy and there were tears shimmering in her eyes. "She says we need time apart." She got up from the table and grabbed a tissue and dabbed at her wet cheeks. "I've never felt like this before, Sandy, and I don't know what to do to fix it."

Sandy gasped and looked at her slightly protruding belly. "It moved!"

Laurel dropped down and put her hands on Sandy's stomach. Her despair momentarily overshadowed. "I don't feel anything."

"It stopped."

"What did it feel like?"

Sandy thought a moment. "I don't know. It sort of…fluttered. Do you think that's normal?"

"I'm as experienced at this as you are. Your guess is as good as mine."

"There it goes again," Sandy said as she covered Laurel's hands and pushed them firmly against her stomach.

"I still don't feel anything."

"It wasn't my imagination. It was fluttering. I guess the baby is too little to kick hard enough to feel it from the outside."

Laurel sat back on her heels. "I guess so." She wanted to ask again how her sister could give up that precious little life that was growing inside her, but they'd already been through that same argument many times. Sandy's mind was made up, and Laurel had resolved to stop giving her grief about it. She got up and returned to her seat across from Sandy. "Are we gonna play cards or what?"

"Oh, Nicole…" The rookie looked up from the paperwork she was filling out to see Sergeant Singer approaching. "Chief Waxman wants you to wait and see him this morning."

*Oh, God.* "Did he say why?"

"No. He should be here soon."

"Okay, I'll be here." Nicole watched Debbie walk away. *What does he want? Is it about work? Did I do something wrong? Maybe it's about Jim. It can't be time for another hiking trip, can it? Please let it be about Jim and nothing else. Could it be about Laurel? No. He's never even mentioned her to me, and she wouldn't go to him about what's going on with us. It has to be about Jim.* Despite her internal pep talk, Nicole nervously finished her paperwork as the minutes ticked away. The clock moved far too fast for her liking, and before she knew it, she was knocking on his office door.

"You wanted to see me, Chief?"

"Come in, Nicole. Close the door and have a seat."

*Uh-oh.* Closing the door almost never bodes well, and Nicole felt her heart rate increase. "Um, is something wrong?"

The gray-haired man smiled and gestured at the empty chair. "You're off duty, Nicole. You can call me Mark." He reached for his coffee mug. "I bet you're wondering why I asked you to stay. I'll get right to the point. Every Sunday, my family has a get together at my brother's house, and I wanted to invite you and Jim to come. I feel like Jim is one of my boys, too, and the rest of the family would like to meet him." He took a sip while she processed his request. "Nicole." He chuckled. "I'm not inviting you to a firing squad, so don't look so scared. The boys will be there, so Jim will have someone to hang out with, and since you know Laurel and Sandy, it only makes sense to invite you, too."

"It's very nice of you to offer..." she began, completely ready to give him an excuse why she couldn't go.

"Good, then it's settled." He smiled broadly and set the mug down. "I'll put directions to Brian's house in your mail slot."

*Oh, no, no, no. This isn't happening.* "Um, Mark, I'm sure Jim will have fun, but..."

"You bowl with the girls, don't you? Think of it as bowling with better food. Casual dress is fine. We don't stand on formalities."

Realizing there was no way to politely refuse his request—order, actually—Nicole reluctantly nodded. "Should I bring something?"

"Just yourself and Jim will be fine," he said. "I have a ton of paperwork to get at, and I'm sure you want to get home. Have a nice day."

"You, too, Chief."

"Hi."

Laurel looked up from the pile of tack she was cleaning, surprise evident on her face. It had been months since Nicole's last visit to the stable, and she had come to believe that the closeness they once shared was lost forever. "Hi, yourself. I didn't expect to see you here."

Nicole looked down. "I know. I just needed to talk to you."

Laurel put the saddle soap down and waved her in. "You can always talk to me, Nicole. I hope you know that."

Nicole flopped down on a bale of hay, resting her elbows on her knees. "I've been trying to give you your space," she said. "I miss this." She gestured at the stall. "Spending time here with you. Just talking and everything."

"You're always welcome," Laurel said, joining her on the bale. "I've missed you coming here, too." She patted Nicole's knee. "So what did you need to talk about?"

"Your uncle invited Jim and me to your family supper on Sunday."

"He what?"

Nicole winced at the tone. "I'm sorry. I tried to turn him down, but he is the chief, and…well, he just didn't seem to want to take no for an answer. Laurel, he's been so good to Jim." She looked down at the floor. "I don't want to make you uncomfortable."

Laurel sighed. "You know what makes me uncomfortable? This distance we have now. Look, you've told me how you feel, and I respect that. I want to be friends, though, and that can't happen if we don't spend any time together. A few minutes between frames at bowling don't count." The truth, which she would never admit to Nicole, was that she missed her terribly and welcomed any opportunity to spend time together. If that meant keeping her feelings hidden, so be it. A little time with Nicole was better than no time. "Besides, your buddy over there has missed you, too." She jutted her chin in Cheyenne's direction.

"She likes me because I give her extra carrots."

Laurel shook her head. "She likes you because you're a kind, caring woman…and because you give her extra carrots." She smiled at the smile her words had caused. "Please, Nicole, let's spend time together again. I really miss our friendship."

Nicole nodded. "Me, too."

"You're not wearing that," Nicole said.

Jim looked down at his T-shirt emblazoned with a popular heavy metal band's logo. "Why not? Mark said casual was fine."

"First of all, it's about thirty degrees out there. Second, I'd rather you made a better impression on Laurel's parents. Your gray sweatshirt would be better."

Groaning, Jim plodded back up the stairs. "Just because you've changed about fifty times already doesn't mean I have to," he said. "You really think Sergeant Sexy cares what you wear?"

"And don't call her that," she yelled up to his retreating form. Crossing the living room, she opened the closet door and studied her reflection in the mirror. *Pale yellow blouse and chinos. Not too casual, right? Maybe I should go with a nice sweater over it. Dangling or studs? Necklace or not? What's Laurel going to wear?* She agonized for several moments before donning her favorite stud earrings and a bracelet made of interlocking silver links. A quick spray of perfume and she reluctantly agreed she was ready. "Come on, Jim. Let's go."

"You know, you're awfully bossy today," he said when they met in the hallway. He had changed into the gray sweatshirt and to her surprise, replaced his ratty sneakers with semi-polished black shoes. "I'll bring the sneaks in case we get into a game of football or something," he said when he noticed her gaze.

"Can I help with the dishes?" Nicole asked when Laurel and Sandy stood and began collecting plates.

"You're company, dear," Elizabeth answered as she linked her arm through Nicole's and led her into the family room. "Laurel and Sandy will do them. It's their turn tonight."

Nicole glanced wistfully at the door that her friend had disappeared through. Laurel's family was very nice, but there were a lot of them, and it was a bit overwhelming. At least the men had adjourned to the playroom in the converted basement, and the kids were off doing whatever kids do when they get together. "Dinner was very nice, Mrs. Waxman. Thank you."

Elizabeth smiled. "I'm glad you came, Nicole. I've heard so much about you and Jim that I almost feel like I know you." She dropped

Nicole's arm and walked to a high table that stood behind a gaudy flower print couch. She picked up a bottle and turned back to Nicole. "Would you care for some wine?"

"That would be nice. Thank you." Nicole accepted the proffered glass and took a sip. A piano across the room caught her eye, and she walked closer to get a better look. It was a baby grand, and she ran her hand reverently across the smooth surface.

Mark's wife, Hanna, appeared at her side. "Beautiful, isn't it?"

Nicole nodded and took another sip of her drink. "I've always wondered what it would be like to play a grand piano. A baby grand is the next best thing."

"You play?"

"I haven't played in a long time. I'm sure I'm pretty rusty."

Hanna motioned Elizabeth over. "Did you know she plays?"

"No, I didn't." Elizabeth took the wine from Nicole's hand and gestured toward the piano. "Please, won't you play for us?"

All eyes in the room turned to her expectantly, and Nicole reluctantly sat at the piano. "I don't know about this. I really don't play very well."

"Don't worry, my dear. They're used to hearing me plunking away. Anything would be an improvement."

Everyone laughed, and Nicole felt some of the tension ease out of her body. It had been so long since she had sat at a piano that her fingers tingled with anticipation. "Okay," she said and began to play.

"Why do you always get to dry?" Laurel asked as she put the last dish in the dish drainer. "I hate dishpan hands."

"Rank has its privileges, and besides, you could wear gloves."

Laurel grabbed a towel and dried her hands. "I hate the feel of rubber gloves, and the way my hands sweat in them they get just as wet as they do in the dishwater. I just wish Ma would come out of the dark ages and get a dishwasher."

Sandy laughed. "Why should she spend good money on a dishwasher when she has you?" She twirled her damp dishtowel and smacked Laurel on the ass.

Laurel's towel began to spin as she followed her shrieking sister from the room. Once in the dining room, the sound of the piano filled her ears, and she stopped and cocked her head to listen. "Wow, Ma's improved."

Sandy listened, then shook her head. "I don't think that's Ma."

They walked in the direction of the sound and found that it was Nicole who was playing. Laurel leaned against the doorway and watched her play. She didn't try to hide the adoration that shone clearly on her face as she gazed upon the woman who had stolen her heart. The song was lovely, and as she listened, she realized there were so many things about Nicole that she didn't know. Wanted to know. She swallowed a lump in her throat and wondered if Nicole would ever give her the chance to find out.

Laurel walked into Sandy's office and dropped down in the chair across from her. "This better be good, Sis. I had a trail ride scheduled this morning."

Laurel watched Sandy get up and close the door. She noted that her belly was blossoming with the new life she carried. It was clear she wouldn't be able to keep the baby a secret much longer.

Sandy returned to her desk and pulled something from the top drawer. She grinned as she handed what appeared to be some kind of picture to Laurel.

"What is it?" Laurel asked as she turned the picture every possible way but could not discern what it might be.

"Your nephew."

Laurel looked again. "You're kidding."

Sandy snatched it back and returned it to her drawer. She leaned back and placed a hand on her stomach. "I'm going to keep him."

Laurel's mouth dropped open, and she jumped up and rushed around to pull Sandy in for a hug. "What made you change your mind?" she asked as she straightened up and sat on the edge of Sandy's desk.

"I tried not to, I really did, but I couldn't help falling in love with him." She gazed down at her belly. "Every time he flutters inside me, I love him more."

"If you're happy, I'm happy. And for the record, I think you'll be a great mom."

"You really think so?"

Laurel grinned. "I really do."

"I'm glad you think so because the prospect of becoming a mother scares the shit out of me."

When are you gonna tell Ma?"

"Sunday. I'm going to put the picture in her Mother's Day card."

Laurel laughed. "I can't wait to see her face. She's gonna love it." She patted Sandy's belly. "I'm going to spoil you rotten, little man."

"Oh, no," Sandy corrected. "I'm not raising a spoiled brat. He's going to be perfect."

Laurel laughed again. "We'll see." She stood and walked to the door. "Don't you go giving her the card until I'm there."

Sandy shook her head. "Of course not. You've been my partner in crime all along. I wouldn't leave you out."

"Just wanted to make sure." Laurel left Sandy's office with a grin on her face. It had felt so good to laugh. She hadn't been doing much of that lately. She glanced at her watch. The group was already gone, but this news was worth missing the trail ride.

"Hey, stranger, how's life been treating you?"

Laurel turned at the sound of the familiar voice to see her old friend Don Colter striding toward her. Her grin broadened. Don had been her field training officer when she joined the force. "I can't complain, Don. How about you? Still with Putney Enviro Industries?"

He nodded. "I retire in fifty-nine days, but who's counting."

"I thought you'd never retire."

"Margie and I decided to buy a motor home and have some fun before we cash in our chips. Her brother had lots of plans for when he retired, then went and had a stroke before he got to do anything. Made us realize that we're not getting any younger. We want to do our traveling while we're healthy enough to enjoy it."

"They have a candidate yet for your replacement?"

"You interested?"

"I might be."

"If you're serious, I'll talk to the boss about you."

Laurel realized she was serious. She loved Nicole with all her heart, and nothing was ever going to happen between them as long as things stayed the way they were. "I'd appreciate it." They continued to talk for a few minutes, but Laurel's mind kept returning to the possibility of a new job. It would remove all the obstacles in her way for a relationship with Nicole.

Laurel sat on the bench next to Nicole and opened her locker. No one else was around, and it seemed like a good time to mention her meeting with Don Colter the day before. He'd called her less than an hour later to say that Putney Enviro was definitely interested in talking to her about the job. He was pretty confident that if she wanted the job, it was hers. She cleared her throat. "I had an interesting conversation with Don Colter yesterday morning. We go back a long way. He was my FTO when I joined the force."

"It's hard to think of you as a fumbling rookie. You're my idea of the perfect cop."

Laurel shook her head. "I wish."

Nicole grinned. "I just calls 'em as I sees 'em."

Laurel returned the smile. "Okay, I'll accept the compliment. Thank you." She pulled off her work shoes and stuck them in her locker. "Anyway, I was talking to Don, and it seems he's retiring as head of security from Putney Enviro Industries soon, and he wanted to know if I'd be interested in taking his place." She looked back at Nicole. "I'm considering it."

Nicole's mouth dropped open. "You can't be serious."

Laurel stood and unzipped her pants. "Dead serious."

"What will your family say?"

Laurel shrugged and continued to strip out of her uniform. "My dad will be disappointed. He thinks I'm going to be Presson's first female chief."

Nicole straddled the bench and leaned closer. "Please think about this, Laurel. You were born to be a cop."

Laurel pulled on her Levi's. "You don't think I should pursue this job?"

Nicole shook her head. "Being a cop is in your blood."

Laurel's heart sank. She was disappointed that she was receiving no encouragement from Nicole. Perhaps this relationship was more one-sided than she had realized. She sat back down and pulled on her sneakers. "I guess you're right." She grabbed her backpack and started for the door, her mood darker than it had been. "Gotta run," she said over her shoulder and disappeared through the door.

Foster & Miller

# Chapter Fifteen

L aurel pulled Sandy into the kitchen. "You still planning on going through with it?"

Sandy nodded and pulled a blue pastel envelope out of her purse and handed it to her.

Laurel opened it and pulled out a card. Sandy had glued the sonogram picture to the card and underneath it read: *The first of many pictures of your grandson, Douglas Brian Waxman.* Laurel tucked it back in the envelope and smiled. "I can't wait till she sees it."

"What are you girls whispering about in here?" Elizabeth asked as she walked into the kitchen.

"Nothing," they said in unison as Laurel's hands flew behind her back.

Elizabeth narrowed her gaze at Laurel. "Are you hiding something behind your back?"

Laurel slipped the card to Sandy, then pulled her hands out to show they were empty.

Elizabeth turned her eyes to Sandy. "I wasn't born yesterday. I know you've got it now."

"Busted," Laurel said as the sisters looked at each other and burst out laughing.

Sandy held up the envelope and grinned. "It's just your Mother's Day card."

"Is that all? Then why were you hiding it?"

"I was just waiting for the right time to give it to you. That's all."

"What's wrong with now?"

"I wanted to wait until the rest of the family was here."

Elizabeth's eyes narrowed. "What's so different about this card that you have to wait for the rest of the family to be here?"

Laurel looked at Sandy. "Give it to her now. She can share it with them later."

Sandy grinned and handed over the envelope. "Happy Mother's Day, Mom."

Elizabeth took the card and shook her head. "I swear, such a lot of fuss over a simple card." She opened it and gasped as her hands flew to her mouth. She looked at Sandy. "A grandson? I'm going to have a grandson?" She didn't wait for an answer and pulled Sandy in for a hug. "Congratulations, sweetheart. I didn't even know you were seeing anyone. When are you going to bring him over so we can meet him?"

Sandy glanced at Laurel, then back at their mother. "I'm not. He doesn't know about the baby."

"You're not going to tell him?"

Sandy clenched her fists, certain her mother would not be pleased with her answer. "He was just a vacation fling. I wouldn't know how to find him even if I wanted to."

Elizabeth reached out and patted her cheek. "Don't worry, baby. Dad and I will be here if you need us."

Sandy smiled at the unexpected support and her hands relaxed at her side. She knew her mother would be pleased about the baby but expected her to blow up at the news that there was no father in the picture.

Elizabeth looked at the picture again and her grin widened. It was clear she could hardly contain her joy at the impending birth. Rushing from the room, she called out, "Brian! Brian, we're going to be grandparents!"

Nicole looked at her watch and sighed. Would this night ever end? She turned on the window defroster as the windshield wipers of her cruiser tried unsuccessfully to keep up with the downpour that had started a few minutes before.

Her thoughts momentarily went to Laurel and the distance that had developed between them the past few months. Headlights coming at her brought her back to the present, and she honked her horn and swerved to avoid a head-on collision with a car that had drifted into her lane. Her car spun out of control on the slick pavement and crashed through the guardrail, tumbling down the steep incline, rolling twice before coming to rest at the bottom.

The driver's window had broken out and rain poured in, mixing with the blood running down Nicole's face. She tried to stay awake, tried to stay focused. She reached for her shoulder mike, but blackness engulfed her before she could call for help.

*"Unit S109."*

Laurel grabbed the mike. "S109, go ahead."

*"S109 respond to Highway 496, just past the Porterville cutoff. Report of a motor vehicle accident with injuries involving Unit 105."*

Her gut clenched, her hand shaking so badly she could barely hold the mike. "S109 en route."

*"Unit S109, be advised we now have a report of possible entrapment. L14 is also responding. Fire and EMS units not yet on scene."*

"S109 clear."

Laurel turned on her lights and siren and flipped around. A thousand scenarios flooded her mind, all involving Nicole and a mangled police cruiser. She fought to push them away. She couldn't do her job if she lost control. She gripped the wheel as she took the turn onto 496 too fast and the cruiser fishtailed for a moment. "Fuck! I don't have time for this."

She brought the car back under control and drove through the pouring rain until she saw a car with its headlights on parked on the shoulder next to the broken guardrail. She parked behind it. There was no sign of Nicole's cruiser until she reached the edge. The cruiser was at the bottom of the embankment, the headlights giving off an eerie glow in the heavy downpour. She saw a man standing by the car waving his hands frantically to get her attention.

"We need help down here," he shouted.

Laurel grabbed her flashlight and first aid kit and started down. "Please, God, please, God," she chanted as she climbed down the rain-slicked embankment, nearly falling twice before reaching the bottom. Once at the bottom, she rushed to the car and shone her flashlight on Nicole's face. Blood flowed freely from a long gash above her right eye, and she wasn't moving. She tried to pull the driver's door open, but it wouldn't budge. The back door wouldn't open either, and she ran around to try the other side. "Fuck!" she screamed, and pounded her fist on the roof of the car in frustration.

Laurel leaned in the broken driver's window, but the noise from the storm made it impossible to hear whether Nicole was breathing. She held her breath while she felt for a pulse, relieved when she felt something. It was weak, but it was there. Nicole was alive.

"I fell asleep," a voice said, and Laurel turned to the sound. "I heard a horn honking, and it woke me up. She swerved to miss me and rolled down the hill." He started to pace back and forth as if in a daze. "I'm so sorry. So sorry."

"Go back to the road and wait in your car. Someone will take your statement later." He didn't move and she gave him a shove. "Go!" She turned back to the car and grabbed the first aid kit, pulling out a gauze pad to push against the gash on Nicole's head. Rain was pouring in the broken window, and Nicole had started to shake. Laurel wasn't sure if it was from shock or the cold, but she knew she needed to do something. She pulled off her jacket and wrapped it around Nicole as tears streamed down her face, only to be washed away by the heavy rain. She gently patted Nicole's cheek. "Wake up, honey."

The sound of sirens caught her attention, and she glanced up to see the EMTs appear at the top of the slope and start down. She picked up Nicole's hand and pressed it to her lips. "You only have to hang on a little longer." She stroked a pale cheek. "Don't you dare leave me," she said in desperation. "Please, baby, stay with me."

Laurel watched them load Nicole into the ambulance and drive away, her fists clenched tightly at her side. She silently cursed the job that kept her here, when all she wanted to do was climb in with Nicole and never leave her side.

It was almost an hour before Laurel finished taking the other driver's statement and completed the accident report. An hour that felt like an eternity. The storm had let up by the time she left, and she made good time on the trip to the hospital. She entered the emergency room and went directly to the door that led to the examination area. She pushed the button on the wall and waited for someone to buzz her in. It seemed to take forever for the automatic door to swing open and she rushed inside, her eyes frantically scanning the room for any sign of Nicole.

"Are you here about Officer Burke?" a voice behind her asked, and Laurel spun around to find a short, stocky woman she recognized from previous visits to the ER.

"Yes, can I see her?"

The woman nodded and pointed to a small room not far away. "She's in there. Someone should be here soon to take her upstairs."

Laurel stopped short when she saw Nicole's battered face in the harsh lights of the emergency room. Her face was black and blue, and there was a bandage over her right eyebrow and another on the side of her head.

The flesh that wasn't bruised was deathly pale. IV tubes ran from her arm to a bag that hung from a rack by her bed. It took all of Laurel's strength not to break down again. She slowly walked to Nicole's side and picked up her hand, pressing it to her lips. "I love you," she whispered.

Nicole groaned and Laurel leaned down and stroked her cheek. "I'm here, baby, you're going to be okay." She watched as Nicole's eyes opened and tried to focus.

"What happened?"

"Your car rolled down an embankment. You're in the hospital."

"My head hurts." Nicole tried to move and pain radiated through her shoulder and chest. She squeezed her eyes shut and fought against the tears that wanted to fall. "I don't remember. Why can't I remember?"

A distinguished man in a white lab coat walked in and looked down at her. "I see our patient is awake." He smiled. "I'm Dr. Richmond." He took Nicole's hand. "Squeeze."

Nicole complied.

"How many fingers am I holding up?"

"Two."

"Good." He pulled a small flashlight out of his pocket and flashed the light in each of her eyes, watching the pupils react.

"What day is it?"

Nicole tried to think. Was it Thursday? Her lip trembled. "I'm not sure."

Dr. Richmond nodded. "You've got a concussion. Loss of memory and confusion are common symptoms. You've also got some pretty good bruising from your seat belt. I expect you're going to be pretty sore for a week or two."

Nicole's stomach picked that moment to revolt, and she barely had time to lean over the edge of the bed before she vomited.

Nurses appeared out of nowhere, and her bed was rolled aside and the mess cleaned up. "I'm sorry," Nicole managed to get out before she vomited again.

"It's okay," one of the nurses said as she handed Nicole a small plastic tub in case she needed it again.

The other nurse handed her a glass of water. "Rinse, honey. It'll help."

Nicole rinsed and spit in the plastic tub. "Ugh." She took another mouthful and spit again. She felt a little better after getting the foul taste out of her mouth. Her gaze fell on Laurel, who was across the room trying to keep out of the way of the bustle of activity around her. Nicole was embarrassed that she had made such a mess, and it was even worse knowing that Laurel had witnessed it.

She was aware of someone speaking and turned back to see Dr. Richmond making notes on her chart as he talked to one of the nurses.

The doctor set the chart down and patted her hand. "Your CT was negative, but you lost consciousness for quite a while. I'm afraid you're going to be our guest overnight, Ms. Burke. We'll do another CT tomorrow, and if it's still negative, I'll release you to go home."

Laurel heard Jim before she saw him. It was clear from the panic in his voice that he was losing it. She understood why. He lost both parents to a car accident, and now his sister had been in one. She rushed out of the room to calm him down before he saw Nicole.

"Jim," she called, and he turned to the sound of his name. His eyes were red, and it was clear he'd been crying.

"Is she..." Jim broke down and couldn't finish the question.

Laurel wrapped her arms around him, and he squeezed back in a death grip.

"Nicole's going to be okay. She's got a concussion. Other than that, she's got some cuts and bruises that look worse than they are. She'll be pretty sore for a while, but the doctor thinks she's going to be fine."

"You sure?"

Laurel nodded. "Nicole was unconscious for a while, and they want to keep her for observation. She'll probably be released sometime tomorrow."

If anything, Jim's grip on her tightened, and Laurel couldn't take a breath. He finally let go and scrubbed his wet face with his hands again. "I'm sorry."

"Hey, there's nothing to be sorry about." She looked past him and saw Mark and smiled in relief. Jim didn't need to be alone right now.

"Can I see her?"

Laurel nodded. "They'll be moving her upstairs to a room soon, but she's still down here. Come on, I'll show you." She led the way to the small room, and they stood together by Nicole's bed. Her eyes were closed, and Laurel could not tell if she had fallen asleep or if she was just resting.

"Oh, Nickie."

At the sound of Jim's voice, Nicole's eyes fluttered open. A halfhearted smile was all she could manage. Jim looked scared and she tried to reassure him. "It's not as bad as it looks, honest."

Jim nodded, afraid to speak for fear he would lose it again, and he didn't want to do that in front of Nicole. With all that had happened to her, she didn't need to worry about him, too.

Nicole opened her eyes, then squeezed them closed again. Bright light streamed in through the window, and she shaded her eyes with her hand before opening them again. She glanced around the small room and noticed that Laurel was sitting in a chair by her bed, her head and arms resting on the bed as she slept. Nicole smiled at the sight of her beloved friend, her thoughts momentarily taken away from the pain in her body and the cotton dry feel in her mouth. She glanced at the bedside table that held a cup of inviting water and thought a moment, trying to decide if reaching for the water was worth the anticipated pain it would cause. Deciding it was, she attempted to sit up and groaned.

Laurel was awake in an instant. "Are you okay?" she asked as she stood and moved closer to the head of the bed.

Nicole nodded but continued to hold her sore shoulder as it changed from a sharp pain back to the dull ache that would be her companion for the next couple of weeks. "I'm okay, I just moved wrong."

"Do you need anything?"

Nicole indicated with her head the water on the bedside table. "My mouth is so dry."

Laurel pushed the button to raise Nicole's bed to a sitting position before handing her the water. "You should have asked me to get it for you."

Nicole took several long sips of water before answering. "You looked so peaceful I didn't want to wake you."

"Don't do that again. If I'm here, ask me. I don't want you hurting yourself." Laurel took the glass and placed it back on the table. She fussed with Nicole's pillow and was tucking the covers in around her when Debbie Singer walked through the door.

"Hey, Nicole, what's with rolling your car downhill in the rain? You into extreme sports?"

Nicole chuckled. "You should try it sometime," she indicated her surroundings, "and you, too, can enjoy these deluxe accommodations."

"No, thanks, sweetie. I'll leave the fun stuff to you adrenaline junkies." She handed Nicole a teddy bear dressed as a patrol cop. "Officer Bear is here to keep you company, so you won't miss the gang back at the station."

"Oh, Deb, I love her."

"Her, huh."

"Of course it's a her. You don't think I'm going to be cuddling with a him, do you?"

Deb slapped her palm against her forehead. "What was I thinking?" She patted Nicole's hand. "How're you feeling?"

"Not too bad." She winced as she reached to place the bear on the chest by her bed. "I should've said, not too bad as long as I don't move wrong," she clarified. "The doctor said I can go home this afternoon, but he won't let me go back to work for a week, then it's going to be light duty for another week." Nicole grimaced. "I hate desk duty."

Laurel grinned when a pretty chocolate-skinned nurse pushed a wheelchair into the room. "Time to go."

Nicole stood up gingerly and smiled. "I am so ready to get out of here." She sat in the wheelchair and reached for the bear that was sitting on the edge of the bed. "You ready to go home, Boo Boo?" She made the bear nod, then looked over at Laurel, who had gathered up two plants that friends had brought. "Home, Jeeves."

Laurel led the way out of the building and across the parking lot while the nurse pushed the wheelchair. The bright sunlight intensified the contrast between Nicole's pale skin and the bruises on her face, and Laurel thought again of how close she had come to losing her.

She stopped at her truck and placed the plants in the back and hurriedly opened the passenger door. She turned to help Nicole, but she was already standing. "Do you need any help getting in?"

"I think I can make it okay." Nicole climbed in and waved goodbye to the nurse. She steeled herself as she watched Laurel walk around to the driver's side of the truck. Laurel had been so attentive and caring, never leaving her side while she was in the hospital. It made her heart ache thinking about what they could never have. It was clear that she needed to make Laurel understand that she didn't need her help. It would just get Laurel's hopes up again, and Nicole didn't want to hurt her more than she already had.

"You all settled in?" Laurel asked as she slid behind the wheel. Nicole nodded and Laurel continued. "Good. We'll make a quick stop at the pharmacy, and I'll run in with your prescription. I can go back and pick it up later."

"I don't want you to have to make a trip back to the pharmacy. It makes more sense to turn it in and wait."

Laurel shook her head. "You need to be home resting. The doctor said you should take it easy the next couple of weeks and get plenty of rest."

"I'm sure there's a place we can sit while they fill my prescription. I'll be fine."

Laurel reluctantly agreed, and they stopped together to pick up Nicole's medication. It was only about a thirty-minute wait, and they were soon pulling in to Nicole's driveway.

Jim must have been watching for them because the front door burst open, and he ran to open the truck door for Nicole. "Are you hungry?" he asked as he took her hand to help her out of the truck. He didn't wait for an answer. "I made that lasagna you like so much." He glanced at Laurel. "There's plenty. I bought the large one."

Nicole really didn't have much of an appetite and would have preferred something light, like soup, but he'd gone to so much trouble that she didn't have the heart to hurt his feelings. "That sounds great."

Jim grinned and took her arm to help her to the house. Nicole didn't want to appear too needy in front of Laurel and pulled her arm away. "I'm okay, really. I can walk by myself."

"I just wanted to help."

Nicole ruffled his hair. "I know, but what I really need is for you to get my plants out of the back of the truck and carry them in for me."

Jim grabbed the plants and ran to open the front door for Nicole. Laurel smiled as she watched him and turned to Nicole. "Does he have an off switch?" Nicole laughed and the sound was music to Laurel's ears.

Laurel stretched out on her bed, but she knew sleep would not be coming anytime soon. She hadn't been home since Nicole's accident, and it felt good to be in her own bed, even if she couldn't sleep. In fact, the only sleep she'd had since the accident was a couple of hours while she leaned on Nicole's bed.

Seeing Nicole's bleeding body in that car had shaken her badly. She shuddered. The fear had been paralyzing. *Nicole could have died.* Even though she knew that Nicole was going to be fine, she couldn't get the image out of her mind. She loved Nicole with all her heart. Why couldn't she get her to understand that? To believe that she was in it for the long haul and would never hurt her the way that Rita had. Tears started running down the side of her face and into her ears.

"Fuck." She got up and went to the bathroom for a cotton swab to dry her ears. She tossed the swab in the trash and splashed water on her face. Crying wasn't going to solve anything. The accident reaffirmed the reality that none of us is immortal, that a life can be snuffed out in an instant. She couldn't let another day go by without doing something to fix the distance that had grown between her and Nicole.

She walked back into the bedroom and picked up the business card she had placed on the nightstand a few weeks before. She glanced at the clock. Too late for him to be in his office, but she could leave a voice mail. She punched in the number and waited for the tone. "Don, it's Laurel Waxman. If that job's still open, I want it. Could you set up an interview, so I can come in and talk to someone? Really appreciate it. Bye."

Laurel handed Arman Danko the envelope and stood mutely while he pulled out the letter and read it. He dropped it on his desk and looked at her. "I don't know what to say." He picked up his pen and absently tapped it on his coffee cup. "I'm sorry to lose you." He stood and walked around the desk to where she stood. "Nothing I can say to change your mind?"

Laurel shook her head. "Afraid not. I've been thinking about this for a long time. Don Colter is retiring at the end of the month, and they've offered me his job. It's a big jump in pay. I'd be crazy not to take it."

Arman stuck out his hand. "Good luck, Laurel. You know I'd never stand in the way of your advancement."

"Thanks."

Foster & Miller

# Chapter Sixteen

Nicole finished up her paperwork and started for the locker room to collect her things. She hated being stuck on desk duty and couldn't wait to be back in her cruiser again. Desk duty sucked. She saw Sandy approaching and noticed that her pregnancy was really starting to show.

"I need to talk to you," Sandy said, and Nicole could see by the stern look that it was something serious.

"Sure."

"Not here, in my office." Sandy turned abruptly and walked away.

Nicole hurried to catch up, worry etching her features. She couldn't imagine why Sandy needed to talk to her. Something was not right. They didn't work together, so it wasn't likely to be about work. That left the family. Panic suddenly overwhelmed her. *Laurel. Something's happened to Laurel.*

Sandy held the door open for her, then slammed it shut when she entered. "She loved being a cop. Now that's gone. I hope you're happy."

"What's happened to her, Sandy? You're scaring me." Nicole's heart was pounding as possible scenarios flashed through her head. *An accident? A shooting?* Surely she'd have heard if something like that had happened. "Is she all right?"

"Physically, she's fine, but she hasn't been all right since the day she met you."

"I don't understand."

Sandy walked to her desk and picked up a piece of paper, tossing it at Nicole.

Nicole bent and picked it up. She was stunned to see that it was a letter of resignation. Not just any letter of resignation. It was Laurel's.

"She's a great cop, Nicole. How could you take that away from her? You should have been the one to quit. Not Laurel."

Nicole's jaw dropped open. She was speechless. "I...I didn't know."

Laurel was surprised to open her door and find Nicole standing on her doorstep. She smiled and stepped back to let her in. The smile soon faded when she took in the grim look on Nicole's face. "What's wrong?"

Nicole marched past her without saying a word. Laurel closed the door and followed her into the living room. She grabbed her arm and pulled her around to face her. "Are you going to tell me what's wrong or not?"

"How could you do this?"

Laurel's brow wrinkled. "How could I do what? Help me out here."

"You can't quit."

"How did you...oh, Sandy."

Nicole nodded and paced back and forth. "You're a good cop. How can you give it up?"

"Maybe I want more from life than just being a good cop."

Nicole stopped pacing and stood toe to toe with Laurel. "It's because of me, isn't it?"

"You know I was offered Don's job at Putney Enviro. It's a lot more money and great benefits. I'd be a fool to turn it down."

Nicole crossed her arms over her chest. "And if I remember correctly, you turned them down."

"They sweetened the offer, and I changed my mind."

"I won't let you quit because of me."

Laurel shook her head. "Why does everything I do have to be about you?"

"Sandy seems to think it does, and before long, everyone at the department will, too. They'll hate me for it."

"I'll tell them it's not true."

"They won't believe you."

Laurel blew out an exasperated breath. "What do you want me to do?"

"Tear up that letter of resignation."

Laurel turned and walked to the kitchen and pulled a beer out of the refrigerator. "Want something to drink?"

Nicole shook her head.

Laurel took a large swallow before turning back to face Nicole. "I'm taking the job."

"Why do you have to be so stubborn?"

"I'm stubborn? Isn't that a little like the pot calling the kettle black?"

Nicole threw her hands up in the air. "I give up." She turned and started for the door.

"Why are you so mad?" Laurel asked as she watched her go.

Nicole paused with her hand on the doorknob and looked back over her shoulder. "I know how much being a cop means to you. No matter what you say to the contrary, eventually you're going to resent me for making you give up your job."

"I won't resent you. And for the record, you didn't make me do anything. I'm a big girl, and I'm doing this for me. Is that so hard to understand?"

Nicole sighed, then she was gone.

Laurel leaned back and closed her eyes. This wasn't the reaction she'd hoped for when Nicole found out about the job. She had pictured her face lighting up with joy that there were no longer any obstacles to their relationship. "I'm gonna kill you, Sandy," she said as a tear made its way down her cheek.

Laurel stormed into Sandy's office and slammed the door. "Who the hell do you think you are going off on Nicole like that? You had no business telling her I gave notice!"

"She had no business pushing you to quit your job."

"She didn't."

"Bullshit!"

"For your information, she tried to talk me out of it."

Sandy crossed her arms over her chest. "Funny, she told me she didn't know anything about it."

"I told her about the job offer, and she talked me out of taking it. I never told her that I changed my mind."

"You're a good cop."

Laurel nodded. "And I'll be just as good at the new job."

Sandy shook her head and sighed. "You're really going to do this, aren't you?"

"Afraid so."

"What if Nicole tells you to stay?"

"She already did. We had a big fight about it, but I'm not changing my mind. This is important to me."

Sandy stood and walked around her desk and sat on the edge. "Okay, Sis, it's your life, your decision. I won't mention it again."

Laurel's anger had been defused, and she sat on the edge of the desk next to Sandy. "Thanks. I know this seemed to come out of the blue, but I've been thinking about it for a long time. It's what I need to do."

Sandy patted her sister's leg. "I hope it works out for you. I really do."

Laurel put her hands in her pockets. "I hope so, too." She sighed. "It has to."

Nicole walked to the kitchen and opened the refrigerator for the third time that evening. She didn't know why she was doing it. She wasn't hungry. She wanted…something, but it wasn't food.

She closed the door again and sighed. Jim was next door helping his friend Rob rebuild the engine of an old clunker he'd picked up for almost nothing, and Nicole longed for someone to talk to. She had only seen Laurel once a week at bowling since she started the new job, almost a month before. She ran her fingers through her hair. Could it only be a month? It felt like forever.

Nicole was so deep in thought that the doorbell ringing startled her, and she jumped. She hurried to the door and found Laurel standing on her doorstep and her breath caught. "Hi." Laurel looked nervous, and Nicole stepped aside to let her in.

"I hope I'm not disturbing you."

"No, come on in." Nicole led the way into the living room. "Would you like something to drink?"

"Sure. Do you have a beer?"

Nicole nodded. "One beer coming up."

Nicole brought a couple of beers and handed one to Laurel. "How have you been?"

Laurel shrugged. "Good. How about you?" She couldn't believe how awkward this felt.

"I've been good, too." Nicole inwardly chastised herself for the lie. She had been anything but good. In fact, she'd been miserable. She watched Laurel take a sip of beer and fidget. She looked uncomfortable. Perhaps she was lying, too, and things were not really that good for her, either.

Laurel cleared her throat. "I know I should have called first, but I was in the area, and I knew it was your night off and took the chance that you weren't busy." She took another sip of beer to bolster her courage. "I thought maybe you might want to go to the Labrys with me tonight."

Nicole sat on the couch and placed her beer on the coffee table. "I don't think that's a good idea."

"Why?" Laurel asked. "You said we could stay friends, but you treat me as anything but." She closed her eyes and puffed out an exasperated breath. "How did we come to this..." she paused trying to come up with the right words, "...awkwardness around each other? We used to be able to talk."

Nicole looked down at her hands. She knew most of this was her doing. What had started out as a protective mechanism had hurt them both, but the fear was still there, and she didn't know how to deal with it. "What do you want from me?"

"I want things to be the way they used to be. We were moving toward something good. I want that back. I want a relationship with you."

Nicole listened to Laurel's heartfelt words and didn't know how to respond. Her feelings for Laurel were too raw. Too needy. She had to get past this before she could be friends without wanting more. "I do want to stay friends. I do. But I'm not ready to pick up where we left off. I need more time."

"I'm not trying to seduce you, Nicole, I just asked you to spend an evening with me. What's the harm in that?"

"I just can't." Nicole looked down, unable to keep eye contact. "This is hard for me."

"Why? We don't work together anymore."

"It may not happen now, but eventually, you'll blame me for making you give up being a cop."

"Let me see if I've got this straight. When I was a cop, we couldn't have a relationship because we worked together." Laurel paused for emphasis. "Now, we can't have a relationship because we don't work together? Something is totally fucked up here."

Nicole flinched at the angry tone in Laurel's voice. "You know that's not what I said." She got up and walked to the window and gazed out at nothing. "I can't bear the thought of seeing the resentment in your eyes."

Laurel crossed the room and grabbed Nicole's shoulder, pulling her around to face her. "You've got us stuck between a rock and a hard place, and I don't know how to fix it. Doesn't it matter to you that I like the new job? That I have no reason to be resentful?"

"Do you miss being a cop?"

"Sure, sometimes."

"I rest my case."

Laurel threw up her arms in exasperation. "What I resent is you telling me how I feel." She crossed the room and pulled the door open. "You obviously don't know me very well at all." She looked back over her shoulder. "Maybe it is better that we're not together. With your uncanny ability to look into the future, I'd never be able to keep any secrets." With those parting words, she walked out and slammed the door behind her.

Nicole crumpled onto a chair, tears starting down her face. She fumbled in her pocket for her phone and found a number in her address book and punched the speed dial. "Deb, this is Nicole. I need you to find a replacement. I won't be bowling anymore."

Laurel placed the saddle on Cheyenne's back and reached under her belly for the cinch. A car pulled up alongside her tack shed and she stepped around the corner of the shed to see who it was.

"I was hoping you'd be here," Debbie said as she got out of the car. "I couldn't get you on your cell, and I needed to talk to you before bowling tonight."

Laurel frowned. "What's up?"

"That's what I'd like to know. What's going on with Nicole?"

"Nothing that I know of. Why?"

"She called me last night and told me we need to find a replacement. She's quitting the team."

Laurel grimaced. "Fuck."

"Did you two have a fight?"

"What goes on between Nicole and me is none of your concern, Deb. Now, if you'll excuse me, I've got a date to go riding." She grabbed Cheyenne's reins and started to walk away, stopping short when she saw Debbie flinch at her curt tone. "I'm sorry. I've got a lot on my mind right now." She ran her fingers through her short hair. "It's just that I've told you a million times, Nicole and I aren't lovers. Maybe now you'll believe me."

They were interrupted when a very striking woman rode up on a large palomino gelding. She had long black hair braded into a single plat down her back. "You ready, Laurel?" she asked, then noticed Debbie. "Oh, I'm sorry, didn't know you were busy."

"No, it's okay." Laurel nodded at Deb. "Sharon Kulp, Debbie Singer." Laurel looked at Debbie. "I'm sorry, Deb, but I've got to go. Sharon and I have a date to go riding." She swung herself into the saddle. "See ya later," she called, then they were gone.

Jim walked into the kitchen and found Nicole sitting at the table still in her sleep shirt and socks. "Why aren't you ready? Don't you have to leave right after dinner?"

"I quit the team."

Jim frowned. "I thought you really liked being on the team."

"I don't anymore, okay?"

"Hey, don't bite my head off. I just asked a simple question." Jim pulled a tray with two TV dinners out of the oven. "Mark called while you were asleep. He said Saturday is Laurel's birthday, and they're having a party at the family gathering on Sunday. He invited us to come."

"No."

Jim placed the tray on top of the stove to cool a minute. "I thought you'd want to go, so I accepted for us."

"Well, you thought wrong. You shouldn't have accepted without checking with me first. What's the matter with you?"

"Geez, Nickie, chill. I didn't think it would be such a big deal." He pulled back the foil on his dinner and placed it on a hot pad on the table. "What's wrong? You and Sergeant Sexy have a fight or something?"

"Nothing's wrong, and stop calling her that!"

Nicole turned in her paperwork and started for the locker room. She hadn't been sleeping well lately and was dead tired. All she wanted to do was get home and collapse. Debbie Singer fell in step beside her, and they walked down the hall together.

"We sure could have used you last night," Debbie said to Nicole as she pulled open the locker room door. "The sub sucked big-time, and on top of that, Laurel was off her game."

"I'm sorry, but you know I was only supposed to sub until Candice's thumb healed. It was never meant to be a long-term thing."

"I know, but I don't have to like it." Debbie sat on the bench and pulled off her shoes. "The Public Works team is in last place. They never beat anyone, and they skunked us." She shook her head. "You know Candice doesn't think she's going to be bowling for a long time, if ever. Every time she tries, her hand swells up. She thinks it healed wrong."

Nicole opened her locker. "Who subbed last night?"

"Linda from day shift."

Nicole shook her head. "I don't think I know her."

"The only thing you need to know about her is that she can't bowl. It was pathetic."

"Come on, cut her some slack. I didn't bowl very well when I first started, and I improved. I'm sure she will, too."

Debbie shrugged. "I stopped by the stable yesterday to see Laurel." She looked over at Nicole. "Have you met the woman she's seeing?" Deb didn't wait for an answer. "She was there, and all I can say is, wow. She's gorgeous."

Nicole pretended that the news didn't bother her, but it did. Her heart started pounding, and she couldn't breathe. It was bound to happen sometime, but that didn't make it any easier to take. And it happened so fast. It was only a couple of days earlier that Laurel was pressuring her to take their relationship to the next level. Was she seeing this woman even then? Nicole frowned. It didn't matter. Laurel was moving on and that's what she wanted, wasn't it? Then why did she feel like someone just ripped her heart out? "I'm glad she found someone," she forced herself to say. "Laurel deserves to be happy."

Nicole grabbed her backpack and started for the door. The last thing she wanted to do was talk to Debbie Singer about Laurel and another woman.

Nicole didn't want to go home, so she drove to the Shop and Go market to buy a large bag of carrots. It felt right to make a stop at the stables to see Cheyenne. She parked her car beside Laurel's tack shed and grabbed the carrots. Laurel was at work, but somehow stopping here the way she used to made her feel closer to her lost friend.

Cheyenne nickered when she saw Nicole and she smiled. "Hi, sweetie. I'm sorry it's been so long since I visited." She opened the stall gate and stepped inside, and Cheyenne gently nudged her chest. "I know. I've missed you, too."

Nicole pulled the bag of carrots from behind her back and opened it. She laughed when Cheyenne caught the scent and lipped at the bag. "Yes, I brought carrots. You know I wouldn't forget your treats." She gave the mare the first carrot and watched her chew contentedly. She sighed. She'd missed this.

She glanced around the stall and knew that Laurel must have been here early that morning. The straw was clean and tidy, and there was still a bit of hay in Cheyenne's feed box. The thought that Laurel had been here so recently brought a tear to her eye.

She stepped closer to the mare and wrapped her arms around her neck, burying her face in Cheyenne's mane. "How did everything get so fucked up?" she choked out through her sobs. "I know it's all my fault, and she probably hates me." Nicole let go and wiped her face on her sleeve. "I guess I can't blame her for finding someone new, but it hurts."

Cheyenne nudged at the bag again, and Nicole gave her another carrot. "It doesn't take much to make you happy, does it, sweetie?" She broke up the rest of the carrots and tossed them in the feed box on top of the hay. She patted Cheyenne's jaw and sighed. "I don't think I'll be back again. I'm sorry for that." She gave the horse one more hug and turned to leave. "Take care of Laurel for me," she said and was gone.

Laurel pulled the stencil off the wall and stepped back to view her handiwork. She had spent a good deal of the day working on the nursery for Sandy's baby, and unicorns now danced across the baby blue wall under a colorful rainbow.

It had been a lot of work, but it was worth it, and she smiled thinking how surprised Sandy would be when she saw the room. She glanced at her watch and realized she didn't have much time to clean up the mess before her sister got home from work.

Laurel stuck the stencils in a bag and gathered up the roller and paint cans and hurried out to her truck to stash them out of sight. It had been a busy day, and she needed to keep busy. Work kept her mind occupied, so she didn't dwell on Nicole.

She had just closed her door when Sandy's car pulled in to the parking space next to her. Laurel glanced at her paint-spattered hands and wished she'd had time to clean them before Sandy got home. She stuck her hands in her pocket and grinned as her sister got out of her car.

"Why do I get the feeling you're up to something?" Sandy asked as she came around the car to join her sister.

Laurel feigned shock. "Innocent little me?"

"Innocent, my ass."

"You cut me to the quick, sister dear. Can't I visit without being up to something?"

Sandy shook her head. "Not with that Cheshire cat grin plastered all over your face."

They walked together to Sandy's apartment, and as soon as the door was opened, Sandy sniffed the air. "What's that smell?"

"I don't smell anything."

Sandy dropped her purse and started walking in the direction of the odor. "You're a terrible liar. Smells like fresh paint to me."

Laurel rushed around her and stood in front of the nursery door. "Close your eyes."

"What?"

"Just do it."

Sandy dutifully closed her eyes, and Laurel took her hand and led her into the room.

"Okay, you can open them now."

Sandy gasped when she saw the colorful wall. "It's beautiful!" She pulled Laurel in for a hug. "Thank you." She studied the wall again and started laughing.

"What?"

"It's just you."

"Me?"

"I mean the horses. Someone else might have picked bunnies or bears, but with you, it's always horses."

"Unicorns. They're unicorns."

"So the horses have horns. They're still horses, and it looks amazing." She looked at Laurel and winked. "Now all we have to do is assemble the crib."

"We?"

Sandy squared her shoulders in determination. "Yes, we. I'm going to help."

Laurel raised an eyebrow. "This I gotta see."

"I'll read the directions to you. You'll see, it'll be very helpful."

"Okay," Laurel said as she went into the living room to collect the large box. "You're in charge of directions." She stood the box up and motioned for Sandy to get on the other side. "You push and I'll pull."

Together they maneuvered the awkward box into the nursery. "Where do you want it set up?" Laurel asked as she began pulling pieces out of the box.

"Over there," Sandy said, pointing to the wall opposite the mural. "I want him to have a good view of the unicorns."

Laurel nodded and tossed the instructions at Sandy. "I believe you have a job to do." She examined the pieces and started lining them up. "This shouldn't take long," she said, and began assembling the crib without waiting for Sandy to decipher the directions.

The baby started kicking, and Sandy grabbed Laurel's hand and pressed it against her belly. "Can you feel him?"

Laurel grinned and a look of amazement spread across her face. "It felt like he kicked, then rolled." The kicking stopped and Laurel dropped her hand. "It's funny how things turn out."

"What do you mean?"

Laurel sat on the floor and crossed her legs. "I'm the one who always wanted to have children."

Sandy dropped down beside her. "You will, and our children will be close. You'll see."

Laurel sighed. "I want to have a family with Nicole." She looked longingly at the mural on the wall. "She doesn't want me."

"Ah, Sis, you can't see into the future. When you least expect it, the right woman will come along and sweep you off your feet. She'll make you forget all about Nicole."

Laurel shook her head. "She's the one."

"I know you think that now, but—"

"Stop!"

"I'm only trying—"

"I don't want to hear it!" Laurel was angry, and she slammed her hand down on the crib box. Why couldn't Sandy understand how much she loved Nicole? This wasn't an infatuation. "You just don't understand."

Sandy watched Laurel's anger turn to despair and reached out for her hand, squeezing gently. "I want to understand."

A tear slipped down Laurel's cheek, and she brushed it away. "I really thought when I left the department that it would change things for us, you know?" She looked down and picked at the paint on her hands. "I can't get her to believe that this change was a good one. That I'm happy with the way the new job is going." She looked up, a defeated expression on her face. "She thinks I'm going to forever hold it against her for giving up being a cop."

"And aren't you?"

Laurel glared at her sister. "Not you, too!" She shook her head. "Being a cop was my job, not my life. I was a good cop, but I never intended to stay a cop forever. You and Dad are the lifers in this family. I thought you, of all people, knew that."

"You're really serious about this, aren't you?"

Laurel nodded. "I was so sure she felt the same about me. That she'd come around once I started the new job." She sighed. "I guess I was wrong on all counts." Another tear started down her cheek and she wiped at it with her shirtsleeve. "I just love her so damn much." Laurel pulled one side of the crib closer and picked it up. "Let's get this thing put together," she said, effectively closing the subject.

# Chapter Seventeen

Nicole was tired as she opened the door to the parking lot and almost ran into Sandy coming in to work. She smiled. "Sorry. I almost ran you down."

Sandy just glared at her and started to push past. It was simply the last straw. She didn't understand why Sandy had always had it in for her, but she was too emotionally distraught to put up with this shit any longer. She grabbed Sandy's arm and turned her to face her. "Why don't you like me? What have I done to you?"

"I don't dislike you, Nicole, but I hate what you're doing to Laurel."

"I know Laurel told you we were never lovers. Why won't you believe her?"

"Oh, I believe her. But you led her on. Made her think something was going to happen, then pulled the rug out from under her. Do you have any idea how much she's hurting?"

"I'm sorry she's hurting, but I'm hurting, too. And for the record, I didn't lead her on. We were friends. That's all."

"You keep telling yourself that, but you and I both know it isn't true."

Nicole released Sandy's arm, but stepped closer. "You've had it in for me almost from the start."

"I know my sister. I saw all the signs that she was heading for trouble. I saw the way she looked at you. The way she treated you. I warned her she was going to get hurt, but she wouldn't listen. I wish to God she had."

"Believe what you want to believe," Nicole said as she turned and walked away. "I've got to go." Laurel wasn't hurting as much as

191

Sandy thought. Didn't she know that Laurel had found another woman to fill the void?

"I'm not going."

"Ah, come on, Nickie, you have to come."

"No, I don't."

"I already accepted for us. Mark's expecting us to come to the birthday party. We have to go."

"I didn't say you couldn't go, but I'm not going."

"What will I tell them? It's Laurel's birthday. She's your friend, not mine."

"I just can't see her right now."

"What's going on with you two?"

Nicole glared at him. "Nothing's going on."

"Now tell me something I believe."

Nicole turned and marched away. "The subject is closed," she called over her shoulder as she disappeared up the stairs.

Her parents' long driveway and the street in front of their house was parked full, and Laurel was forced to park quite a way down the street. She climbed out of the truck just as her Uncle Mark and his family pulled up and parked behind her. The boys ran on ahead, and Mark and Hanna joined Laurel on the sidewalk.

"How's life treating you?" Mark asked as he gave her a one-armed hug.

Laurel shrugged. "Wouldn't do any good to complain."

Hanna laughed and accepted a hug from her niece. "No, but sometimes it makes us feel better."

They continued down the sidewalk and up the rose-lined walk to the front door, the sweet fragrance wafting up around them.

"Are you planning on giving Sandy a baby shower?" Hanna asked just before they reached the door.

Laurel nodded. Sandy's baby was one of the few things she had to look forward to anymore, and she was planning on going all out for her sister and the baby.

"How would you like to have it at my place?" Hanna asked. "It's a lot bigger than yours, and Elizabeth is less likely to think she's in charge if it's at my house."

Laurel grinned. "That'd be great, Hanna. Thanks."

Hanna returned the grin. "Good. We'll have to make some time soon, so we can get everything planned."

"I'm open anytime," Laurel said. "Just let me know when you need me, and I'll be there."

The door opened, and Mark popped his head out. "Are you two coming in?"

"Yeah, yeah," Laurel said and stepped inside. She jumped back when a chorus of "Happy Birthday to You" assaulted her ears. She was truly surprised. The Waxmans weren't big on birthday parties, except for the youngsters or major milestones, and Laurel didn't consider thirty-three to be a major milestone.

Sandy put a party hat on her head and handed her a beer. "Were you surprised?"

"Totally." Laurel pulled the little hat off her head and handed it back to Sandy. "Whose idea was this anyway?"

"Mine. I thought you needed some cheering up, and nothing is cheerier than a rousing party."

Brian pulled Laurel into his arms and kissed her on the forehead. "Happy birthday, honey."

"Thanks, Dad," she said as they linked arms and walked through the crowd of assembled Waxmans. A blond head caught her eye and she smiled. Nicole's brother Jim was across the room talking to Mark's boys. Her heart started pounding, and she started for him. If Jim was here, Nicole must be here, too.

Jim grinned as she approached. "Happy birthday."

"Thanks." Laurel's eyes scanned the many faces mingling together in the room. "Where's Nicole?" she asked as her eyes stopped searching and settled on him.

Jim said, "She couldn't make it," but the look in his eyes told her all she needed to know. Nicole didn't want to see her anymore. So much for staying friends.

The night was warm, and Laurel drove with the windows open. She needed to do something, anything, to take her mind off Nicole and the endless void the loss of their friendship had left in her life. She turned on Hoover, intending to go talk to Sandy, but a glance at the clock on the dash changed her mind. No reason Sandy should be wakened at two in the morning just because she couldn't sleep.

Laurel turned on Willow and kept on driving with no destination in mind. Anything was better than going back to an empty apartment. Tears obscured her vision, and she pulled over and parked. *Why did I have to kiss her after the chess game? Everything was fine until that night.*

Laurel wiped angrily at the tears and opened the door. She climbed up on the hood of the truck and leaned back against the windshield, watching as the full moon momentarily disappeared behind some passing clouds, darkening the night to match her mood.

A faint sound off to her left caught her attention and she cocked her head to listen as her eyes scanned the darkness. The moon emerged from its shroud, softly illuminating a figure walking toward her in the distance. She couldn't verify if it was male or female, but the broad shoulders led her to believe it was male. She could see that he pushed a shopping cart, and she filed it away as another homeless person in search of a place to bed down for the night.

The mystery solved, she leaned back against the windshield and studied the moon once more. There was a halo around it, and she remembered that someone had once told her that a ring around the moon meant it would rain within twenty-four hours. She absently wondered if that was true as she glanced over to see the man—she was sure now—with the shopping cart turn and start up the overpass that crossed the highway up ahead.

Laurel sat up and watched intently as alarm bells went off in her brain. He was close enough for her to see what appeared to be a cinderblock in the cart. She slipped off the hood of the truck and walked silently toward the retreating figure. Her fingers found the phone clipped to her belt, and she quickly dialed 911.

*"911, what is your emergency?"*

"This is Laurel Waxman. I'm at Willow and the Turner overpass. I have a possible suspect for the cinderblock murders. Suspect male, wearing Levi's and a dark shirt. He's pushing a shopping cart that may contain a cinderblock."

*"Do you have a visual on him?"*

"Yes, I do."

*"I'm sending two units to your location. Keep him in sight, but stay back, Laurel. Do not pursue. Repeat, do not pursue."*

Laurel closed her phone and continued following the suspect. She had no intention of standing back and allowing him to drop a block on another unsuspecting victim. She stayed out of sight as best she could, walking among the trees that lined the road. That would only work until she reached the overpass. From then on, she would be out in the open.

She reached the last tree and paused to check her watch. *Where are they?* From her vantage point, she could see the highway below and the suspect, who was standing near the center of the overpass. No cars were approaching, and she decided to stay put until absolutely necessary.

Suddenly, cinderblock guy's stance grew straighter, and she followed his gaze down to the highway. Headlights in the distance signaled that necessary had indeed arrived. At highway speeds, the car would be under him in less than a minute.

She started to move when he lifted the block out of the cart and shifted to the correct lane to wait. She grabbed her phone as she ran and dialed 911. "This is Laurel Waxman. Can't wait for backup any longer. Car approaching, have to intercede. She flipped the phone closed before they could answer and picked up her speed.

Out of habit she called, "Stop, police!" and he glanced in her direction.

"No!" he screamed, and held onto the block. "It has to be done." He widened his stance and held the block over the side. "It has to be done!"

Laurel stopped and held her hands up to show they were empty. "Please, put the block down and let's talk about this."

He shook his head and continued his chant. "Hold your water, it has to be done. Don't let it out, or they'll get you, too. It has to be done."

Nothing he said made any sense and Laurel was certain she was dealing with a wacko. She started running again and tackled him just as the car was about to drive under them. The block fell, and Laurel prayed that she had thrown his timing off and he'd missed.

The man hit the ground hard and didn't move. Laurel thought he'd been knocked out and pulled out her phone to call in again. At that moment, Nicole's cruiser pulled in behind her. She put her phone back and called out, "He's unconscious, call for medical transport. This guy's a wacko."

Then his arms started flailing and he screamed, "No, no, no! I can't fail. I held my water! No!" He scrambled to his feet and started to run, but a police cruiser pulled across the road and blocked his path. John Decker got out of the car and the man fell to his knees, sobbing. "I held my water."

Laurel went to the rail and looked over to see what damage the block had done. The car was nowhere in sight, but the block was broken in several pieces.

John had the guy cuffed and locked in the back of his cruiser by the time Nicole got there. "I called for medical transport. Do we still need it?"

"Oh, yeah," Laurel said as she joined them. "This guy's off his rocker. He needs some serious evaluation."

John patted Laurel on the shoulder. "Good collar, Waxman. You should still be on the force."

Nicole crossed her arms over her chest in an 'I told you so' manner and lifted an eyebrow. "See? I'm not the only one who thinks you made a mistake. It's not too late to change your mind. They'll take you back. Rumor has it you're a woman with connections."

Laurel's hands balled into fists, Nicole's attempt at humor lost on her. It was hard to keep her cool with adrenaline still pumping through her body from the scuffle with cinderblock guy. "I have no intention of ever coming back, but if I did, my record would speak for me, not my family." She looked at John. "I'll stop by the station on my way home and give my statement." With that, she turned on her heels and was gone.

Nicole left roll call and stopped by Debbie Singer's desk to say hello before heading to her cruiser. She wanted to ask Debbie about Laurel but didn't want to sound like she missed her too much. Her brief encounter with Laurel the week before when they'd arrested cinderblock guy had ended on a sour note she wished she could take back, and she couldn't help feeling guilty that she had once again sent Laurel away with a bad taste in her mouth.

Debbie smiled when she saw her coming. "Hey, Nicole. How ya doing?"

"Okay, I guess. How about you?"

"Can't complain."

Nicole laughed. "Wouldn't do any good anyway."

"Ya got that right." Debbie picked up a pencil and tapped it against her coffee mug. "Have you talked to Laurel lately?" she asked, and Nicole had an excuse to talk about Laurel.

"No. I guess she's been busy, what with a new job and a new girlfriend." Nicole cleared her throat. "How is that going, by the way?"

"What? The job or the girlfriend?"

"Both."

"She hasn't mentioned Sharon, so I don't know how that's going. She likes the job, though."

Nicole's ears perked up at the name. She knew Sharon Kulp and her husband owned the stables and that Sharon was an old school chum of Laurel's. "Sharon Kulp?"

Debbie thought a moment. "Yeah, I think that was her last name."

Nicole felt her knees go weak, and she leaned against Debbie's desk to steady herself. "Sharon's not her girlfriend. She's straight."

Debbie's brow wrinkled. "Are you sure?"

Nicole nodded. What a fool she'd been, but then she'd had no reason to doubt what Debbie said. "Sharon's an old friend of Laurel's. She and her husband own the stable."

The phone rang, and Debbie picked it up; Nicole used that as an excuse to end their conversation. She didn't know whether to be glad at the news or not. Secretly, she was relieved that Laurel wasn't seeing anyone, and that made her feel guilty. When Debbie told her about the new girlfriend, she'd tried to convince herself that she was glad that Laurel had moved on, but it wasn't true.

Nicole hurried to the cruiser, her stomach tied in knots. She wished she could call Laurel right now, but what could she say? I'm sorry for being such an ass and ruining our friendship or any chance we had at a relationship. No, it was too late for that. She had already burned her bridges where Laurel was concerned. She had repeatedly pushed her away, and the final straw had been not showing up at her birthday party. She was certain she had sent Laurel a clear signal that she didn't want to see her anymore. Nicole sighed. She was sure that she was the last person Laurel would want to hear from.

"Thanks for coming, Bob." Laurel gestured at one of the two guest chairs in her office. "Please, make yourself comfortable." She watched the sandy-haired man pull out a chair and sit down.

"How long have you worked with Jay Peters?"

Robert Smart thought a moment. "I think it's about four years now."

"Do you know him well?"

"Well enough." Robert frowned. "What's this about?"

"Just some irregularities we're trying to track to the source."

Robert stood up and placed both hands on the edge of Laurel's desk. "Look, Jay's a good guy. He doesn't need this garbage."

"I'm not attacking him, just trying to identify the source of the problem. Believe me, we're talking to everyone connected to the Green Screen project. I'm not singling him out."

A knock sounded at the door and Laurel called, "Come in."

The door opened, and Julie, her administrative assistant, popped her head in. "I know you wanted your calls held, and I'm sorry to disturb you, but the reception desk just called. There's someone down there asking for you."

"I'm in the middle of something, can't it wait?"

"I guess the guy said it was urgent that he see you."

Laurel nodded. "Thanks, Julie." She picked up the phone and dialed the reception desk. "This is Laurel Waxman."

"Yes, Ms. Waxman. There's a James Burke waiting to see you."

Laurel's heart rate sped up. Why would Jim come here to see her? Unless...Nicole. Something had happened to Nicole. "I'll be right there," she said and slammed down the phone. "I'm going to have to cut this short, Bob." She ushered him to the door. "Thanks for your time."

Laurel didn't wait for him to answer but rushed down the hall past the elevator and opened the door to the stairwell and started down. There was no way she had the patience to stop at each floor and wait for passengers to amble in.

By the time she reached the lobby, she had worked herself into a full-blown panic attack. "Jim," she said as she approached the teenager. "Is everything okay?"

Jim's expression was somber, which scared her even more.

"I need to talk to you. It's about Nickie."

"Is she okay?"

"Can we go somewhere private?"

Laurel didn't want to wait for an answer, but she nodded and led the way down the hall to a door that opened into a courtyard with benches surrounding an elaborate granite fountain.

"What's wrong, Jim? You're scaring me."

Jim sat down heavily. "I don't know what happened between the two of you because she won't talk about it. What's going on, Laurel? What did you do to her?"

Laurel sat down beside him and placed a hand on his shoulder. "I swear to God, Jim, I didn't do anything to Nicole except care for her. Too damn much for my own good."

"I don't understand."

"Neither do I." She ran shaky fingers through her hair.

"You had to have done something." He stood up and started pacing back and forth. "She stopped spending time with you. She stopped talking about you. Since then, she doesn't want to do anything fun anymore. She just mopes around the house, and when I ask her what's wrong, she says 'nothing.'" He sat down again. "Can't you apologize?"

Laurel took a moment to pull her thoughts together. This really wasn't a conversation she wanted to be having with a teenage boy. On the other hand, it may be the only way to find out what was going on with Nicole.

"Jim, it's not like you think. I didn't do anything but fall in love with your sister."

"Then what happened?"

Laurel picked at a nonexistent piece of lint on her pants. "She made it clear to me that she didn't want that from me. She said she wants to be friends."

"You sure don't seem like friends anymore. At least not to me."

"Me, either. I hate the distance that's grown between us, but I don't seem to be able to do anything about it."

"This sucks."

"Tell me about it."

Jim turned on the bench and his sad eyes tracked to hers. "I've never seen her this way before, Laurel. It's way worse than when she split from Rita."

"Nicole and I were never lovers. No matter how much I may have wanted it, we never crossed that line. We were friends. That's all."

Jim shook his head. "It was more than that. At least it was to Nickie." He paused a moment to gather his thoughts. "She loves you."

Laurel shook her head. "I wish that were true."

"It is true. You've got to believe me. When you used to call, her face would light up, and she'd walk around with a silly grin just from talking to you." He sighed. "Now she never smiles."

Laurel stood and walked over to the fountain and gazed at the cascading water. *How did things get so fucked up?* She and Nicole had been so close, then everything fell apart.

She turned with a purpose and walked back to stand in front of Jim. "Can you make yourself scarce tonight?"

"Sure. What did you have in mind?"

"I need to talk to her...alone."

Jim nodded. "She usually wakes up around five or five thirty because we eat at six."

Laurel placed a hand on his shoulder and squeezed. "Thanks."

Jim stood. "I just hope you can talk some sense into her."

They turned and walked back toward the building. "Me, too, Jim. Me, too."

Nicole rubbed the sleep out of her eyes and glanced at her watch. It was almost six o'clock, and she wondered why Jim let her sleep so late. She made a bathroom stop and headed to the kitchen for a jolt of caffeine to jump-start her battery. The house was quiet. No TV or CD player blasting as usual. "Jim?" she called as she walked into the empty kitchen. "Where is that kid?" She grabbed her coffee mug and walked to the chalkboard they used to write notes to each other. Sure enough, there was a message scrawled across it.

```
Nickie,
Rob and I are working on a school project together.
I'm eating at his house tonight. Stuff in freezer to
nuke. Coffee's ready.
Jim
```

Nicole poured a cup of coffee and dropped into a kitchen chair. It was going to be a long evening.

She glanced at the refrigerator and tried to work up enough enthusiasm to get up and fix something to eat. Nothing sounded good.

She took a sip of her coffee and wondered what Laurel was doing. She sighed. *Don't go there, Nicole.*

The doorbell rang, and Nicole cursed silently that Jim wasn't home to answer the door. All she had on was an old oversized T-shirt she slept in, which was certainly not fit attire for answering the door. She ran her fingers through her unruly hair and grabbed Jim's barbecue apron from the drawer. Slipping it on quickly, she tied it as she walked to the door. She wasn't expecting anyone and reasoned it must be one of Jim's friends.

Her breath caught when she peeked out the window and saw Laurel standing on her doorstep. She felt guilty about Laurel giving up her job for her, no matter how much Laurel insisted it wasn't true. It made it hard to face her.

She opened the door a crack and peeked out. "Hi."

"Hi," Laurel replied, waiting to be invited in. After a minute of awkward silence, she realized no invitation was coming. "Can I come in for a few minutes? I need to talk."

Nicole really didn't want to be alone with Laurel right now. Especially in her state of undress, but how could she refuse without being rude? "Sure," she said as she backed away from the door. She nodded into the living room. "Make yourself comfortable." She waited for Laurel to walk by, so she could follow her in. Laurel sat on the couch, and Nicole sat across from her on Jim's recliner. "How have you been?"

"Good."

They sat a moment in awkward silence, neither knowing quite what to say. Nicole smoothed the apron across her lap and tucked it down around her bare legs. "How are things going with the new job?"

"Things are going well. I like it a lot."

Nicole leaned forward, her elbows resting on her knees. "You're not just saying that to make me feel better?"

"I wouldn't do that." Laurel cocked her head in thought. "Well, maybe I would, but I'm not."

Nicole raised an eyebrow. "You said you needed to talk to me about something."

Laurel nodded but remained silent. She wasn't sure how Nicole would react but she had to try. If Nicole shot her down again, it would be the last time. It was now or never. "Do you love me?"

The question was blunt, and it took Nicole by surprise. She stumbled over her words. "I...I don't know what to say."

Laurel got up and crossed to Nicole, pulling her to her feet. "Just answer the question. Do you love me?"

Nicole turned away, unable to look Laurel in the eye. "It's not that easy." She tried to pull her hands away, but Laurel's grip tightened.

"Yes, it is. It's exactly that easy." Laurel puffed out an exasperated breath. "I love you, damn it, and you love me!" Her heart was pounding as she pulled Nicole into her arms and kissed her soundly. "Any problems with that?"

Nicole's heart raced and her lips tingled from the kiss. She was stunned Laurel still wanted her after all the pain she'd caused her. "Well, maybe one."

It wasn't the answer Laurel hoped for, and she prepared herself to be shot down again. "And that would be?"

"The kiss didn't last long enough."

Laurel choked back a sob and pulled Nicole into her arms again. "C'mere."

Nicole didn't hesitate, wrapping her arms around Laurel and pressing her face into her neck. "God, I've missed you."

Laurel tightened her grip around Nicole and held on for dear life. She knew if she tried to speak she'd start to cry. Try as she might, the tears started anyway, and Nicole wiped them away with her thumbs.

"I'm sorry for all the pain I caused you. I've been such an idiot."

"It's okay."

Nicole shook her head. "It's not okay, and I'm sorry it took me so long to see it. Thank you for not giving up on me."

Laurel cupped Nicole's face in her hands and pressed her lips to her forehead. "Never." She pulled her back into her arms. "We're together now. Nothing else matters." Her heart was racing as she nuzzled Nicole's neck, nipping lightly with her teeth. She shuddered when she felt the low groan vibrate in Nicole's throat. "I need you so much."

Nicole backed away, taking Laurel's hand, threading their fingers together. She turned and led the way to the stairs, never releasing the hand that clung so desperately to hers.

Nicole paused before opening the door to her room. "Excuse the mess. I didn't make the bed when I got up."

Laurel smiled. "The last thing on my mind right now is whether the bed is made." She pushed Nicole against the wall, pressing their bodies together. "Damn, you feel good," she whispered.

"I can't believe this is happening," Nicole said, her fingers threading through Laurel's hair.

Laurel nuzzled Nicole's neck again. "I've wanted to touch you like this for so long," she murmured before taking an earlobe into her mouth and gently sucking.

"I...oh, God, Laurel..." Nicole pushed Laurel away and fumbled behind her back to untie the apron. The tie stubbornly refused to untie, and she realized in her haste to cover herself she had knotted it.

"Let me," Laurel said, turning her around and working on the knot until it came loose. She gripped the apron and shirt, pulling them over Nicole's head and letting them drop to the ground. She pulled Nicole tight against her, her breasts pushing into Nicole's back. Slowly, her hands trailed up Nicole's body to cup firm breasts. "I want you so much it hurts."

"Then take me."

Laurel pulled Nicole around to face her, bending to take an erect nipple into her mouth.

Nicole threaded her fingers in Laurel's hair and pushed her breast harder into Laurel's mouth. "God, that feels good."

When Laurel's hand slipped down Nicole's body and cupped her sex, Nicole trembled and her breath caught in her throat. She covered Laurel's hand and pushed it hard against her. "Please, love, I need to feel you inside me."

Laurel opened the door to Nicole's room and led her to the bed, gently pushed her down, and straddled her body. Locking her elbows, her upper body hovered over Nicole, her eyes burning with desire.

"Off," Nicole said as she tugged on Laurel's shirt. "I want these clothes off. I need to feel your skin against me."

Laurel nodded. "Don't move. I'll just be a minute."

Nicole smiled and watched Laurel climb off the bed and undress. She had seen her change many times at work, but this was different. She was taking everything off, and she was doing it for her.

Laurel crawled back on the bed and gently lowered herself, so she covered the entire length of Nicole's body.

Nicole's fingertips traced down Laurel's back and stopped on her rounded butt. "You feel so good," she whispered, awed that the woman of her desires was in her bed ready to make love with her.

Laurel groaned and lowered her head until their lips were scant millimeters apart. "Not half as good as I'm going to make you feel," she promised, sealing her words with a kiss.

Nicole's breath caught as Laurel's lips left hers and traveled downward, kissing the valley between her breasts. "Oh, Laurel," she sighed as soft lips mapped their way across her abdomen, leaving goose bumps in their wake.

Laurel slid back up her body, laying her cheek on Nicole's right breast and slowly tracing her fingertips over the other. "So beautiful," she whispered reverently. "So very beautiful."

The need to be with Nicole, to touch and be touched, to give and be given, was overwhelming. "I love you, Nicole. You're all I think about. I can't believe this is happening, that I'm finally touching you. I keep thinking I'm going to wake up and find out this is just a dream."

"If this is a dream, I don't ever want to wake up."

"Me, either," Laurel said, sliding down to close her lips around Nicole's hard nipple. She moaned as her tongue moved over the pebbly flesh. This was Nicole's body she was touching, Nicole's hands on the back of her head. "Nicole...my Nicole."

"Yes." The soft, husky voice inflamed Laurel's soul. "Yours, all yours."

Laurel moved up, claiming Nicole's mouth, their tongues dancing over each other. She wanted to go slow, to take the time to study all of Nicole's body, but her need was too great. She needed to taste her lover's essence, to savor with her mouth and tongue the sweetness of Nicole's most intimate place.

Nicole took Laurel's hand and placed it between her legs. "Now," she begged. "Please."

Laurel slipped a finger between the inviting lips beneath her hand. Nicole was wet and open, so ready for her. "Yes." She scooted down the bed, and Nicole parted her legs in anticipation. "Perfect," she whispered, her mouth watering at the heady scent. She kissed the damp curls and parted Nicole's glistening lips with her fingers. She had dreamed about this moment, fantasized more than once about how it would be, but her fantasy paled in comparison to reality.

"Oh, Laurel," Nicole cried out as her hands clenched Laurel's hair.

Laurel's breath caught. Oh, how she loved to hear the sound of her name coming from Nicole's lips. Her thumb and finger found Nicole's engorged clit and squeezed and stroked it. She smiled at the moan her action caused and did it again, letting her tongue slip out to taste her lover's excitement. "My Nicole."

Laurel's arms tightened around the warm form draped across her chest, a silly grin plastered on her face. *She loves me.* She basked in the warmth of Nicole's body against her own, the feel of velvet skin beneath her fingertips, the scent of their lovemaking still heavy in the air. This was bliss. "I could stay like this forever."

"I wish I didn't have to go to work," Nicole said regretfully. "I need to get up and get ready soon."

"Just a few more minutes," Laurel said, gently rubbing the soft skin of Nicole's back. "I'm not ready to let go of you yet." She let herself enjoy the feeling of everything being very right.

Nicole kissed the breast her cheek rested against. "I never thought I could feel like this." She hugged Laurel close. "I can't even begin to describe it."

"I can," Laurel said. "It's called being in love." She kissed the top of the red head under her chin. "I want to feel your arms around me when I go to sleep and when I wake up."

Nicole pushed herself up and looked into Laurel's eyes. "That sounds like a beautiful dream."

Laurel cupped Nicole's face. "Oh, baby, it's not a dream. I love you. I want us to live together, as a couple and as a family. I know we can make this work."

A tear trickled down Nicole's cheek as she gazed into Laurel's eyes and saw the truth of her words sparkling there. Laurel wanted to make a life with her. She snuggled back down into Laurel's arms. "Sometimes dreams do come true."

# OTHER TITLES FROM INTAGLIO

**Josie & Rebecca: The Western Chronicles**
by Vada Foster & B L Miller; ISBN: 1-933113-38-3

**Misplaced People**
by C. G. Devize; ISBN: 1-933113-30-8

**Murky Waters**
by Robin Alexander; ISBN: 1-933113-33-2

**None So Blind**
by LJ Maas; ISBN: 978-1-933113-44-9

**Picking Up The Pace**
by Kimberly LaFontaine; ISBN: 1-933113-41-3

**Preying On Generosity**
by Kimberly LaFontaine; ISBN: 978-1-933113-79-1

**Private Dancer**
by T. J. Vertigo; ISBN: 978-1-933113-58-6

**She Waits**
By Kate Sweeney; ISBN: 978-1-933113-40-1

**Southern Hearts**
by Katie P. Moore; ISBN: 1-933113-28-6

**Storm Surge**
by KatLyn; ISBN: 1-933113-06-5

**These Dreams**
by Verda Foster; ISBN: 1-933113-12-X

**The Chosen**
by Verda Foster; ISBN: 978-1-933113-25-8

**The Cost Of Commitment**
by Lynn Ames; ISBN: 1-933113-02-2

**The Flip Side of Desire**
by Lynn Ames; ISBN: 978-1-933113-60-9

**The Gift**
by Verda Foster; ISBN: 1-933113-03-0

**The Illusionist**
by Fran Heckrotte; ISBN: 978-1-933113-31-9

**The Last Train Home**
by Blayne Cooper; ISBN: 1-933113-26-X

**The Price of Fame**
by Lynn Ames; ISBN: 1-933113-04-9

**The Taking of Eden**
by Robin Alexander; ISBN: 978-1-933113-53-1

**The Value of Valor**
by Lynn Ames; ISBN: 1-933113-04-9

**The War Between The Hearts**
by Nann Dunne; ISBN: 1-933113-27-8

**Traffic Stop**
by Tara Wentz; ISBN: 978-1-933113-73-9

**With Every Breath**
by Alex Alexander; ISBN: 1-933113-39-1

# Forthcoming Releases

## Revelations
Erin O'Reilly
July 2007

## Away From The Dawn
Kate Sweeney
August 2007

## The Gift of Time
Robin Alexander
September 2007

## Heartsong
Lynn Ames
October 2007

… And Many More

You can purchase other Intaglio Publications books online at www.bellabooks.com, www.scp-inc.biz or at your local bookstore.

Published by
**Intaglio Publications**
P O Box 794
Walker, LA 70785

Visit us on the web:
**WWW.INTAGLIOPUB.COM**